THE SONG OF HELEDD

by

Judith Arnopp

Published in 2018 by FeedARead publishing
Copyright © JudithArnopp
Revised Edition
The author has asserted their moral right under the Copyright, Designs and Patents Act, 1988, to be identified as the author of this work.
All Rights reserved. No part of this publication may be reproduced, copied, stored in a retrieval system, or transmitted, in any form or by any means, without the prior written consent of the copyright holder, nor be otherwise circulated in any form of binding or cover other than that in which it is published and without a similar condition being imposed on the subsequent purchaser.

A CIP catalogue record for this title is available from the British Library.

Covershot: © Captblack76 | Dreamstime.com
Cover design: Covergirl

The eagle of Eli, loud his cry:
He has swallowed fresh drink,
Heart-blood of Cynddylan fair!

Prologue

I dreamed of the eagles long before they came swooping down from their cloudy crags. They blackened the sky, the wind from their wings lifting my hair as they circled with talons extended before settling on the field of death.

Too torn for tears, I waded through my slaughtered kin while pain ripped my heart like a dagger, and when I saw Cynddylan's fallen standard, his torso twisted, his neck broken, his mouth gaping, my step faltered and the world turned dark around me.

I knelt in his blood and tried to close the yawning wound upon his chest but I was too late, he wa s gone. All of my kindred were lost and the Kingdom of Pengwern was shattered. I was left alone. What had I done? Unprotected beneath the vast and empty sky, I threw back my head and screamed a protest to the vengeful gods.

When I woke in the morning and found myself safe in my furs, I flung back the covers to run outside. My playmates tumbled as usual beneath a kindly summer sky while the women spun yarn in the shade of the alder trees. I put up a hand and shielded my eyes from the sun as my brother's hounds came bounding to meet me, leaping up to try to lick my face. I pushed them away.

And then I saw him. My brother, Cynddylan, the King of Pengwern. He was striding across the enclosure with an arm about his companion. I ran to tell him of my terrible dream but, intent on the affairs of men, he waved me away.

He would not listen.

I was just nine summers old then and as I grew to womanhood the dream faded and I forgot it. It was many years later, on the eve of a great battle when I heard again the far off cry of the wheeling eagles, and remembered my dream and knew what was to come.

PART ONE

OSIAN'S SONG

Cynddylan of Powys purple gallant is he!
The strangers' refuge, their life's anchor,

October 644 AD

It all began on the day that my sister Ffreur and I first saw the singer of songs. He came in after supper and filled my brother's hall with his sweet music. The company were entranced, King and commoner alike, and even the dogs ceased worrying their fleas to listen as his voice flowed smooth like nectar, drowning us all in his honeyed lies.

He was a golden man, his hair burnished by the leaping torches and a beard the colour of bees wax curling thick upon his chin. He stood by the hearth, the flames of the fire licking his Midas hair and bewitched us all. I was just a girl, my heart as yet untouched by the beauty of men, but the words of his song filtered deep into my soul and kindled something warm and dangerous in the depths of my belly.

When his song ceased we were all so lost in his art that it took a little time for the murmur of applause to grow. We sat up and looked at each other, blinking in surprise at finding ourselves back in the familiar hall. And then my brother, Cynwraith, the first to recover from the minstrel's spell, rose from his seat and clapped him on the back before leading him to the high table. The handsome poet sat among the men of my kin, flushed and laughing while his platter was piled with food and his mead cup was filled to the brim.

The singer of songs had found favour with the great King of Pengwern and secured his future.

Beside me Ffreur clasped her hands across her stomach, her eyes as bright as the torches, missing nothing. She nudged me sharply in the ribs and laughed at me but I tossed back my hair and ignored her.

'Heledd,' she hissed, 'stop it; your mouth is open. You are almost drooling.'

I closed my lips and wriggled in my seat, the heat of the fire suddenly too great. I wanted to know his name and longed for him to notice me and as I picked up a piece of mutton and glanced at him through my lashes, I pondered how to get closer to him.

When his appetite was sated Cynddylan requested another song and the stranger took his place before the top table again. Every inch of me tingled with anticipation and I sat up straighter, with my chin on my hands and prepared to be enchanted again. The hall fell silent and even the children ceased their noisy games to sit cross-legged on the floor to listen.

He picked up his harp and ran long, white fingers across the strings before his voice engulfed us, ebbing and flowing like clear water over pebbles, turning my skin to gooseflesh.

> *In one year*
> *One that provides*
> *Wine and bounty and mead,*
> *And manliness without enmity,*
> *And a musician excelling,*
> *With a swarm of spears about him.*
> *With ribbands at their heads,*
> *And their fair appearances.*
> *Every one went from his presence,*
> *They came into the conflict,*
> *And his horse under him.*

It was The Song of Urien Rheged. I had heard it a thousand times but never before had it sounded so good. This singer put his soul into his words and the lyrics made my blood run so thick that my heart pumped long and slow. It was agonising to listen to him, as if he knew my deepest, darkest secrets and was about to spill them over the floor. Invisible ties connected us, almost as if he had strung his harp with my heartstrings. It was not something I was strong enough to fight and so I sank my chin in my palm and closed my eyes, blocking the tears as I let his voice caress me and take me where it pleased.

By the time he noticed me I was familiar with every contour of his face and knew intimately how his hair curled into his neck, the strength of his jaw, the sensuous curve of his mouth and the softness of his smile. Then, quite astonishingly, his eyes fell upon me and my heart leapt like a deer in the forest. For a moment he stilled, held fast in my gaze before he continued his song. His fine features mesmerised me, the crowd in the hall seemed to drift away leaving the minstrel and I alone in the firelight, his words and his music exclusively mine. And when the magic ended for a second time and he bowed his head ever so slightly in my direction, I bent my own head in return and I was sure that I saw him close one eye.

I had been prepared since birth for a political marriage, and as the eldest princess of Pengwern, I had always known that my heart was not my own to give. But on that night, while the autumn winds howled about the hall and blew small yellow leaves in beneath the lofty door, I forgot who I was. Without a second thought I dismissed my family and my royal obligation and gave my heart to a singer of songs.

Two

Twilight is a magical time. It is neither night nor day but somehow a time apart, a time when the spirits roam and the gods creep closer to the earth. It is a time of magic. On that night, when the King had retired and the feasting ended, some strange enchantment seemed to draw me from sleep and thrust me unheeding into the perilous future.

I don't know how I knew he would be waiting for me but I ignored Gwawr calling me back to bed and moved in a sort of dream, through the darkness to the place where the yew trees merged at the far edge of the settlement. My feet sped onward. I could not contain them and did not know, or care, where they would take me. Captured by a will stronger than my own, as if compelled by fate, I forgot my years of schooling and my status withered to nothing as I rushed heedless into the future. A decision that would shape all our lives.

Far off an owl hooted and close by I heard a rustle in a darkness that was so complete that I could not see a foot ahead of me. With a thumping heart I slowed my pace and crept forward into the yew tunnel.

It was a favourite place of mine; somewhere that Ffreur and I had loved to play as children, a dark and secret world that smelled of resin and ancient, mystic things. My pace slowed and I lingered in the shadows and did not at first notice the outline of his body moulded to the polished tree trunk. When he stepped forward, bringing my steps to a halt, he seemed to materialise from another world.

Neither of us spoke, it was not a time for words. We both knew that. Both of us were keenly aware that we hovered together on the cusp of fate, governed only by sorcery and our futile mortal words would change or embellish nothing. I raised my eyes to his and he blinked slowly, like a cat and reached out to lightly touch my cheek. I was not afraid. I tucked my face into the warm cup of his hand and moved into the loving circle of his arms.

It was not wrong. We were gifted, one to the other, by the gods and we could not fight it, did not want to fight it. Our union was preordained and so on that chilly autumn night, as the ignorance of my girlhood melted into the heat of his adult fire, I did not tremble.

Afterwards we lay upon the hard ground, wrapped in each other's arms and shrouded by my loosened hair. For the first time my naked flesh pressed against that of a man, for the first time I felt the inexpressible pleasure of consummated love. With his long, white finger he tucked a stray strand of hair behind my ear.
'My name is Osian,' he whispered and the wonderful sound of the word washed inexorably against my heart like the sea against the shifting shore.
'And I am Heledd,' I said and as I said it, he stilled in my arms, his face blanching as he realised the enormity of our act. He had heard of me. Everyone knew of the Princesses Heledd and Ffreur, and Osian was not slow to realise that should our night's work be discovered the penalty would be death. I saw his fears but I was filled with a child's optimism and I laughed gently at them, kissed away furrows from his brow and made him love me again, truly believing that nothing would ever harm us.

Three

The threat of war was never far from us at Cynddylan's hall. My brothers fought a constant battle with neighbouring Kings who coveted our boundaries as well as maintaining the peace within our own jurisdiction. There were ever petty discords and acrimony to be appeased as well as the threat from further off. My younger brothers governed the smaller, lesser Kingdoms in Powys and wherever possible the family sought to secure strong alliances so that when war threatened from outside, the whole of Powys would be prepared and invincible.

I was proud to be the sister of Cynddylan. Since infancy I had watched him stride about his domains, his purple cloak swaying to his heels, his hand on the hilt of the golden sword that had been passed down for generations from father to eldest son. With a man like Cynddylan at the helm the realm flourished. We were a proud dynasty, the kingdom prosperous and our people secure. From all over the land chieftains came to swear fealty and pay tribute to their King and often neighbouring rulers visited to share a feast or celebrate a joining. On those occasions Cynddylan's hall would be swathed in cloth of gold in their honour and the best food was laid upon the tables. In my father's time, and now in Cynddylan's, the hall grew famous for its hospitality and everyone knew that only the best entertainers and the greatest comforts were to be found at the hall of Pengwern.

Two days after I first lay with Osian, when my head was still reeling with the magic of new love, royal guests arrived from Gwynedd. I was busy stitching amber beads onto my tunic; beads that I knew would tremble in the torchlight when I sat at the high table to listen as Osian sang his songs. In those heady days I lived only for him and although war rumbled constantly in the distance I spared little thought for events in the wider world.

Ffreur was beside me, busy embellishing her own gown but I let her have only the lesser gems, keeping the best for myself. I imagined how Osian's face would light up when he saw me in my finery and as I stitched, a warm glow spread across my belly when I imagined how, when we met after dark, he would push the tunic from my shoulders and clamp his hot lips upon my throat.

Impatient for the evening, I snapped off the thread.

'Come, Ffreur,' I leapt to my feet. 'Let us try them on.'

She grabbed up her garments and we set off in the direction of our sleeping bower with Gwawr waddling in our wake, complaining of her sore feet. Aches and pains had no place in my world and I hurried on unheeding of her trials but Freur slowed her step and helped the old woman across the compound. I was too impatient to dally and by the time she and Gwawr crossed the threshold I was already changed and had fastened the jewelled girdle about my waist. I held out my arms and spun around for their appraisal. 'Oh, Heledd,' cried Ffreur, 'how lovely you look. Every eye in the room will be upon you.'

I smiled smugly, knowing she spoke the truth and began to loosen my hair from its bonds. Ffreur picked up the comb. 'Let me brush it, Heledd,' she offered, 'and then you can do mine.'

I sat down and closed my eyes, tilting back my head a little as she gently teased out the tangles. Her touch was gossamer light, making me shiver as goose pimples spread like water across my skin.

The settlement was simmering with excitement and servants rushed, in a hubbub of activity about the brightly lit hall, preparing the tables, plumping the cushions and replenishing the hearth. Supper was not far off and a quiver of anticipation passed through my body at the thought of being with Osian again. I could barely contain myself until the merriment was over and I could sneak away to where he would be waiting, as usual, in the tunnel of yew.

'Has anything happened, Heledd?' Ffreur asked suddenly. 'Do you have a secret? You have that look you used to get when we were children and you were keeping something from me.'

I darted a look at her. Her face was pink and I knew she suspected me. Usually I told her everything but this secret was too big for sharing. It was dangerous and I knew I could tell nobody, not even her. I snatched away the comb.

'Don't be ridiculous,' I snapped. 'Come, it's your turn, sit and let me dress your hair.'

When we arrived at the hall the fiddlers were tuning their instruments, servants wove in and out the company with jugs of mead and trays of victuals and the top table already groaned beneath the weight of food. Mine and Ffreur's chairs stood empty but my brothers were already sprawled in theirs, deep in conversation with two richly clad strangers.

As we approached the men straightened up in their seats and Cynddylan beckoned us to hasten to his side. We walked slowly toward them, conscious of their appraisingly looks and in response I jerked my chin high, at the same time noting their fine garments and noble bearing. They were both strangers and wondering who they were, we stopped at a short distance from the table and executed a graceful greeting as we had been taught.

Pengwern's King stood up. Cynddylan was clad in his best finery, his purple cloak brushed to perfection, a thin band of gold on his brow and a torc as thick as my arm about his neck. He turned and extended an arm toward us.

'These are my sisters, the princesses Heledd and Ffreur, and this is my friend, Cadafael of Gwynedd and his younger brother, Iestyn.'

So this was Cadafael. I had heard of him and his brother. I turned a haughty eye on them and inclined my head slightly. When King Cadwallon, the former ruler of Gwynedd, was slain by the North Umbrian army at the battle of Hefenfelth, Cadafael, a stranger from afar, had usurped the throne from the dead King's infant son.

Ever since that day my brother's relationship with the men of Gwynedd had waxed and waned like the moon and I wondered how long this episode of goodwill would last. My brother was a just ruler, loved and respected by his people but it was said that Cadafael ap Cynfeddw ruled Gwynedd with an iron fist and that loud mutterings of discontent rumbled loudly throughout his kingdom. Obviously, I surmised, he needed my brother's aid to hold on to his usurped crown while Cynddylan sought the alliance with him only to lessen his array of enemies.

I knew Cynddylan was watching us and from the corner of his eye he must have seen the King of Gwynedd sit up in his chair and assess us with his wandering eyes. Placing a ham-sized fist on each knee, he raked up and down my body until I felt I was a weaner being assessed for the pot, but my brother acted as if he had noticed nothing. The Gwynedd King gave a lop-sided smile and it was with great revulsion that I realised that he found me pleasing. His attentions were as welcome to me as a bucket of cold water. I wanted to find favour with no man but the one I loved. As soon as his lips touched the back of my hand, my stomach turned so that I had to suppress a shudder and the kiss ignited an internal storm that was to rage within me for years to come.

Ffreur simpered at the younger man, Iestyn, who leaned forward to engage her in friendly conversation. She smiled as she moved to sit beside him at the top table, her golden head nodding in response to his greeting. Cadafael gestured that I should take my place beside him too but before I did so I darted my eye to Cynddylan to affirm that it was his wish also. And, at his nod, with ice in my heart, I challenged Cadafael's scrutiny, raised my chin and took the empty seat beside him.

The feast was a lengthy one. I sat like a stone effigy as Cadafael plied me with the tastiest morsels from his trencher and bored me with tales of his wonderful Kingdom. His stolen kingdom, I reminded myself, his rebellious kingdom.

The meal dragged on and I did not relish the feast although the rest of the company grew boisterous and loud. My head began to ache. I toyed with a compote of berries and every so often concealed a yawn behind my hand. But at last, when most of the platters were empty and Osian stepped onto the dais, the evening began to improve. I pushed the food away, my heart fluttering like a bag of moths and silently let my love fly toward him across the throng.

He sang a plaintive song of a lone woman, the wife of an exile, pining for her man to return. It was a song full of pain and loneliness and my foolish heart made me feel I was one with the woman, just as lonely as she. Although just a hall full of people separated us, I pined for Osian as if it were an ocean.

Later when the feast dwindled into sleep, and bodies were spread snoring about the floor, I managed to evade Gwarw's summoning call, and crept away, running softly around the perimeter of the settlement, taking the long route to the yew tunnel, careful that none should see me.

As I had known he would be, he was waiting and this time there was no hesitation, no entranced magical exchange of wonder. There was no time for that and we fell upon each other hungrily, hurrying from our clothes and consummating with a reckless passion the lust that demanded easement before it consumed us both.

A crescent moon peeked through the wind-rocked tree tops as he lay stretched out on the ground with me astride him. His hands were cold on my fevered skin and I leaned my head back, the ends of my hair tickling my buttocks, the night air caressing my body while he bucked beneath me like a man possessed.

'Heledd,' he gasped, his face pink with exertion and pleasure. 'Yea gods,' and he rolled me onto my back, buried his face in my neck, riding me onward, possessing me totally, body and my soul.

Afterward, my mind blown away by the ferocity of loving, I lay beside him and watched the stars twinkling through the close linked branches of yew. I wished I could linger all night, inhaling the resin from the trees, listening as his breath slowed, the heat on his body cooled and his pulsing heart fluttered against my ribs. I was young enough to think that the moment would last me forever and that if such a moment never came again, I could live on it and be satisfied by it. Such is the folly of youth.

Four

Freur and I were at our tapestry when Cynddylan summoned us into his presence. We put down our needles and made sure our tunics were clean. Then, smoothing our hair beneath our veils we made our way to the royal bower.

We hesitated at the door but before we had time to make our presence known, the portal was thrown open by the King himself. 'Sisters!' he cried and kissed us both, his lips wet on our cheeks, his welcome so warm and brotherly that we knew the summons was not from the King but an informal meeting with our brother.

He sat us upon heaped cushions, plied us with wine and sweetmeats, his conversation merry but all the while he seemed ill at ease, and a few times he began to say something but stopped, distracted by some small diversion. I knew that a deeper purpose lurked beneath his cheer. We rarely came into his private quarters and I watched him, ensconced in luxury, his every need supplied and wondered how it felt to a King, your people's well-being entirely dependent upon your decisions. For all luxuries that came with it leadership couldn't be easy. I let my eyes stray about the room, noting that the wall hangings were the richest I'd ever seen, the furniture burnished to a deep red hue by the vast fire that roared in the centre of the chamber.

Close to the fireside a dark haired woman strummed a harp. She was young and comely and in my newfound awareness of the lure of love, I wondered if she was Cynddylan's concubine. I felt myself flush as unbidden images of them together crept uninvited into my head and Cynddylan, noticing my wandering attention, sat up to disconcertedly wave her away.

She stopped playing and stood up. I noted her long legs and high bosom as she placed her harp upon its stand and gracefully turned to bow to her King, a curl of black hair escaping from beneath her veil. We were silent until she was gone from the chamber, leaving the three of us alone.

Almost immediately Cynddylan began to pace the floor, his hounds at his heels, his hands clasped behind his back, his head down. At last he stopped, lifted his arms and let them fall again and his dogs sat and looked up at him with their ears pricked as expectantly as ours.

'Sisters,' he began. 'Heledd and Ffreur, my most precious sisters.'

I silently acknowledged the truth of this but Ffreur, ever over-demonstrative, scrambled from her cushions to hug him before linking his arm with hers.

'And you are our most precious brother, Cynddylan.' She beamed up at him and I could see this wasn't helping him as he struggled with some as yet unspoken words. As I perceived that the message he had to impart was important indeed, the first rumblings of dread began to stir in my belly. He disentangled his arm, pressed Ffreur back into her seat and emitted a gusty sigh.

'I have some news which concerns you both.'

Neither of us spoke but waited while he ruffled his hair, placed a hand on his hip and took another deep breath. 'This is not easy, but you both knew it would come one day and well, the thing is … Cadafael, King of Gwynedd is seeking your hand, Heledd and … and Iestyn has asked for you, Ffreur.'

I suddenly felt as if all heat from the room had vanished, the flames abruptly extinguished. I wrapped my arms about my upper body, licked my lips and desperately swallowed my instinctive resistance to his words. I could not give myself away. Cynddylan was right. I had always known this would come one day. Ffreur turned and placed a hand on my knee.

'Oh, Heledd,' she cried, her face pink with joy, 'a double wedding. How lovely that will be.'

My chin threatened to nobble into tears but I was Heledd, I was a princess and Princesses of Pengwern did not cry. They never cried. I fought back the dread, smoothed a smile across my face and squeezed her hand in return although I did not yet have the capacity to speak. My own desires must be thrust away. I would not let myself think of Osian.

Through the pain I lifted my eyes to my brother.

'And when is this double wedding to be?' I asked him, as if my heart were not breaking.

I tried to recall Cadafael's face but all I could remember were his large hands shredding the flesh from the bones of his mutton before placing it between my stiff lips. I had not really paid attention to his face or his bearing and so all that remained was a vague impression of an oversized, grasping man. Why had I found favour with him when my manner had been as frigid as I could make it within the bounds of politeness. How could I ever wed with him? Misery crept upon me like a death shroud and I could not warm myself although, once back in our bower, I wrapped the warmest fur I owned about my shoulders. I waded through so deep a dread that I could not contemplate the future, although I tried to for duty's sake ... and for Ffreur's.

That night at supper my heart was as heavy as a stone and I could not force a morsel between my lips. When the stripped bones were cleared away and the lighter course about to be served the bards had begun to tune their harps. But when Cynddylan banged his fist on the board for attention the music dwindled into discord and the babble of voices lessened to attend the words of their King.

'Good People,' he cried, a cup held aloft in his outstretched hand. 'I should like you to join me in thanks for a forthcoming day of happiness and celebration when my sisters, the princesses Heledd and Ffreur, will be joined with King Cadafael and his brother, Lord Iestyn of Gwynedd.'

A brief lull was replaced by a storm of applause. I summoned a watery smile and blinked away the tears that had been just below the surface all day. When I could bear it no longer I dragged my eyes reluctantly to where Osian stood, unmoving, at the back of the hall.

His jaw had fallen open and his face was drained of colour and my heart broke afresh when I saw, in every curl of his hair and each despairing bead of sweat on his brow, that he was as crushed by the news as I. Across the revelling crowd our souls clasped and as our eyes locked I feared I would drown in his swimming eyes. And then he turned from me and slipped away quietly into the dark.

Ffruer went to her marriage bed blithely, relieved to have been given a husband both young and handsome. I, on the other hand, approached the joining with loathing, unable to accept that those moments with Osian had been our last and that I must give myself to another. Once wed to Cadafael I would be forced to live for the rest of my life on those fleeting happy memories with Osian and I knew now that they would never be enough. On the eve of my wedding day I knew I would crave him for every hour, every minute, every second of every day until the time of my passing.

The dowries cost my brother dear and in the weeks that followed, a fine hoard of precious objects were collected together and piled in the strong rooms. Gold, silver, jewels, tapestries and furs, and in the water meadow grazed a herd of fine cattle that had been recently raided from across the River Taff.

I had always known that marriage would come one day but now the time was here I felt betrayed, cheated by the gods. Why had I been shown the joy of love only to have it snatched away again? It did not seem fair. I no longer found any pleasure in anything and for the first time was truly miserable and wished I was any woman other than a princess of Pengwern.

Ffreur and I, in both body and spirit, were freaðuwebbe, traded by my brothers to forge a treaty of peace between the two Kingdoms. As long as the marriages held, so would the peace and as long as the peace held, so would the marriages and what Ffreur accepted as a blessing, I regarded as a curse.

I knew little then of war. Although the men of our halls rode frequently into battle, Ffreur and I took little interest. Only when someone precious was lost did we mourn and then not for long, for grief sits lightly on the young. Every month some aunt or uncle was laid beneath the sod of Pengwern and just as frequently, the young women were taken in childbed or shortly afterward by the fever. Every adult I knew had suffered the loss of a child and too many tiny hollows marked the resting place of an infant that had failed to thrive in the harshness of our world. We were accustomed to these things, and although we felt the sorrow, we accepted that death was part of life and treated it accordingly. So why could I not accept my duty as a royal daughter of Pengwern? My marriage to a stranger was as inevitable as death, and just as welcome.

Unlike our brothers who had travelled the length and breadth of the land, Ffreur and I had never left the enclosing walls of Pengwern. It was our home, our security, all we had ever known and the prospect of leaving heaped further bitterness upon my troubles.

'At least we will be together,' comforted Ffreur, when she finally came down from her pinnacle of joy and realised I was not happy with the match. 'It would be worse were we parted.'

I nodded absently. 'I will get used to it I expect,' I lied, and hoped that she would never know that, for me, leaving Pengwern was worse than death. It would be better for me to die now than to suffer interminably, perishing in slow, despicable misery.

I had not seen Osian since the night of the betrothals and was not even sure if he remained in Cynddylan's hall. He no longer sang in the firelight but was replaced by a young man with corn coloured hair whose songs did not touch me. As a result, our long suppers became intolerable and the nights long.

And the days were little better. I could find no solace in my young siblings as I had used to and the chatter of even the smallest ones merely jarred my enduring headache. And worst of all, there was no one I could confide in and for the first time in more years than I could count, I craved the comfort of my long dead mother. I was surrounded by kin: uncles, aunts, cousins, brothers, sisters, servants, yet for all that, I was alone and trapped. Helpless.

Five

November 644 AD

It was of the finest cloth and decorated with the richest beads but the gown I wore for my marriage to Cadafael lay heavy on my shoulders. To testify our purity Ffreur and I wore our hair long, a thin band of yellow gold balanced upon our brows and while she had every right to do so, I knew myself to be a hypocrite. But we made a handsome pair; my sister was a head shorter than I and small boned and fair beside my tall, sturdy darkness.

While we were still dressing Cynddylan marched into our bower, loudly demanding to see his fair sisters and, when he saw us, he stopped in his tracks, lifted his arms and dropped them again, pretending he was made speechless by our beauty. 'Well, look at you, Heledd, and you, Ffreur, the finest looking princesses in Powys.'

He came forward planting kisses on our cheeks, his beard tickling as the comforting aroma of horse and leather filled our noses. It was an aroma that no amount of unseasonable bathing could eradicate. Ffreur spun around, thrilled with her new tunic.

'I am so happy, brother,' she reached up, kissed his beard but I stood a little apart, sombre but resigned and trying to pretend it would not really happen.

Cyndyylan, sensing my sorrow, returned Ffreur's kiss before saying gently, 'I would speak with your sister, Ffreur. Go on ahead and we will follow.'

In a great flurry of excited waiting women our younger sister left us alone. I heard her merry laughter as they hurried out into the fresher air. I moved across the room and stood at the brazier, looking down at my hands that I held as close to the flames as I could bear. The day was not cold but sometimes it seemed I would never be warm again. Cynddylan came closer.

'You do not share her happiness?'

I was silent, unable to explain or even to think of a credible excuse. I did not welcome the marriage but I could not tell him so and it did not occur to me to refuse it. My duty had been drummed into me since I was an infant and I knew that my happiness came a poor second to the stability of my homeland. It did not matter that my own heart was breaking. My own needs were unimportant. I had to give myself to the Gwynedd King and saw little point in pretending it could be otherwise but all the same, I could not be happy about it.

When I made no answer Cynddylan cleared his throat, a silent order for me to raise my head and look him in the eye. He was my brother but that role always came second, first and foremost, he was my King. But just for that moment it changed for a short space and I knew that he expected me to speak as openly as if he were not my monarch. It was time to be honest, or as honest as it was wise to be.

'Nay, Brother,' I replied. 'I am sorry, I cannot be happy at this match but you need not fear I will shirk my responsibility.'

His face fell and he took my pink-tipped fingers in his, our faces were level, his cool grey eyes bored deeply into mine.

'Ah, little sister,' he murmured. 'I had no fear of that. There are aspects to marriage you cannot yet know but there is some pleasure to it.'

I dropped my gaze, felt heat glaze my cheek and prayed he would never guess my lack of innocence. 'And I suspect that frightens you but you will be happy in time. I understand our mother was a reluctant bride but she was well content once her young ones came. She was a well-contented woman, wasn't she?'

I nodded, the illicit knowledge of the love I had shared with Osian and how delighted I would be were the match to be made with him, clanging like a bell in my head. The image of him that sprang before my vision; his golden hair, eyes that shone with love of me brought a flaring of pain and moisture stung my eyes. I closed them quickly, trapping the tears and suppressing the misery.

I blinked to clear my vision and tried not to dwell on the memory of those wonderful intimacies. I knew I must soon allow Cadafael similar liberties and my heart quailed at the thought. I envied Ffreur. She was lucky in her ignorance of all that marriage entailed but when I imagined another man's hand where only Osian's had been, or thought of another's lips where his should be, it made my stomach twist with revulsion. I had no idea how I would get through it but in a vain attempt to dispel the fog of negativity, I shook myself and smiled a brittle smile for my brother's sake.

'Of course, Brother, I am just being mawkish. I cling to childhood that is all. The preparations have tired me and I am ungrateful. I should be more appreciative of good fortune when it finds me.'

Fooled by my deceit, Cynddylan cheered up, offered me his arm and we left the bower together. The people of the settlement were already streaming down the hill toward the river where a strange ceremony to a new god that we still but half understood was to be held. We trod the carpet of greenery to the small wooden church of Jesus, whom Pengwern worshipped now, and the gnarled old man in fusty robes that was the settlement priest came out to greet us.

Our King decreed that we must worship this new foreign god but secretly many of our people, and I was one of them, clung obstinately to the old ways, unconvinced by the power of a man-god who had been nailed up by the hands and left to die.

The church had been erected at the old gathering place where the waters burst forth from the land, a place where some said the ancient water sprites dwelt. It was November and evergreen branches had been spread upon the path, both as a wish for fertility and to take up the cloying mud from underfoot. Come spring the naked limbs of the trees would be bowed down with may-blossom but on that cold winter morning they were adorned only with tattered offerings our people had made to the old gods.

The hopes and wishes of Pengwern hung in the branches of those trees, tiny hopeless prayers that had never been granted, and although we were supposed to be Christians now, nobody was brave enough to take the offerings down. I saw a string of shells that I had left there one far off summer in hope that our mother would recover from the fever, and I recognised a braid of ribbon I had tied there just a few weeks ago to beg the gods to save me from marriage and make Osian somehow become mine.

The old gods had not answered, they seldom did, but neither had the new, to whom I had also prayed. And so, it was there, close by the spring in the small wooden church of the new God, that Ffreur and I were joined with the strangers from Gwynedd.

The wedding feast was strident and joyful. I painted a smile upon my face and tried to look happy but I could not join the revel. It was not the same for Ffreur. I sat in isolation and watched her as she wove in and out of the throng, her face growing pinker, her hair slipping from its bonds. She was more than a little drunk on mead and the delight of being a bride but she knew little of the marital act that would follow while I, on the other hand, knew too much. With each passing moment, as the time of consummation grew closer, the horror in my heart at sharing such intimacy with Cadafael grew stronger.

I dreaded being alone with him and tried not to think of the closing of the chamber door, the loosening of clothes, the wrong man touching my body, penetrating my secret places, intruding into my very mind. I felt it would be a betrayal of all the love I had offered Osian and all I had taken. And, more prosaically, I also feared the human indignity of Cadafael's sweaty passion and had no clue as to how I would suffer it.

But suffer it I must but I prayed that my greatest fear of all would not come to pass, for the thing I dreaded most of all was that, at the moment of consummation, he would realise that I was no maid and came to him impure.

If by any means my husband discovered that I was not chaste then the treaty with Cynddylan would be broken and he would cast me off or lock me away. He could have me beaten, leave me to fend for myself, leave me to die. The future security of my people rested on this coming night for if I could not fool my husband into believing that I came to him untouched, the kingdom would be plunged once again into brutal war.

'Come and dance, Heledd!'

Ffreur broke into my maudlin thoughts. She leaned over the table, her bosom heaving with exertion but I shook my head, smiling gently.

'I have a headache.'

It was no lie, my temples throbbed with the drumbeat and my neck ached from holding it so erect. In fact, my entire body was racked from the effort of not simply getting up and running away. I felt like a rat in a trap.

Ffreur plumped into the chair beside me and drank from my cup, her upper lip beaded with perspiration. I envied her such innocent joy. She bit into a piece of mutton and scanned the hall for her new husband who stood with Cynddylan and our brothers at the hearth. She leaned close to me and giggled, waggling her fingers in his direction.

'Iestyn is a fine dancer,' she laughed. 'He lifted me so high I thought he would drop me. Where is Cadafael?'

I shrugged. I did not care so long as he was far from me.

'Don't you like him?' She pulled apart a piece of rye bread and tucked it in her cheek.

'I don't know; we have barely spoken. Do you think it matters in a marriage?'

'What? Liking? Oh yes, I am certain. To live with a man you cannot tolerate would be unendurable. I have never even hoped for love but I think I could find it with Iestyn.'

I looked at her sideways, feeling churlish for my lack of joy.

'Tonight will tell.' I teased, forcing myself not to begrudge her special day and I was rewarded when she flushed as pink as a seashell. She fell quiet for a while and then blurted out.

'Do you think it can be as awful as it sounds? The joining, I mean, it can't be that bad, can it? After all, mother did it … more than once.'

Our mother had borne many children in her time and so had our father's second wife. Our brothers numbered twelve, and six of nine sisters were still living. I remembered the happiness both Mother and our step-mother had found in her children and hoped that they had found as much pleasure in my father's bed. I laughed and pushed at Ffreur's shoulder.

'Maybe she liked it very well and that is why there are so many of us.'

Our eyes met before we burst into simultaneous laughter, drawing the attention of the company, and those nearby cast doting smiles in our direction.

Iestyn put down his cup and came to grab Ffreur's hand, dragging her back to the dancing. As they moved away I saw him whispering in her ear, lifting her hair to leave a wet kiss upon her neck. She tucked her chin down, her cheek dimpling and I looked away, biting my lip, discomfited and made jealous of her pleasure.

'Lady,' came a deep, dark voice. 'I think it's customary that we dance at our own wedding feast. I am tired of talking war with your brothers. We should share the celebration with Iestyn and Ffreur.'

Cadafael towered over my seat but when I stood up we were of a height. He grasped my cold fingers in his hot palm as I allowed him to lead me through the steps. He was light of foot and his touch was gentle. He let his arm trail across my waist and then I felt his warm hand move up and rest upon my shoulder before sliding, dry and calloused, into mine. I had never danced with Osian, my true love, although I had longed to do so, and at the thought my legs began to tremble with a desperate longing for my husband to be somebody else.

As we danced I did not meet Cadafael's eye, although I knew he sought my attention. I kept my head turned away as if I was relishing the enjoyment of the other revellers and as soon as the music ceased, I pulled away.

When the dance ended I caught sight of Ffreur embracing her husband, her body tight against his. She threw back her head, baring her throat as she laughed uproariously at something he said. I wondered how many cups of mead she had drunk to make her behave like that and knew that for me to feel the same it would take several barrels.

Iestyn pulled her close and they kissed, long and luxuriously, exploring each other's mouths, his hands roaming over her body. Her arms wound about his neck as they stumbled together across the floor toward the door to the ladies bowers. There the couple paused and Iestyn spun her around and raised his arm.

'Good night, people,' he cried drunkenly and grabbing her hand, dragged my shameless little sister giggling from the hall.

The company roared with laughter, rolling in their seats, shouting obscenities after the departing couple that would have made a bawd blush. Then they turned back to the business of drinking and the music started up again. With my head down I began to hurry back to my seat but Cadafael grabbed my hand, holding me back.

'My brother has neither patience nor manners it seems but at least his impatience has made it fitting that we retire too.'

I tried not to shudder when he kissed the side of my mouth before leading me to where Cynddylan and Cynwraith supped with the other Lords of Powys.

'We are tired,' Cadafael announced, slurring his words, as if trying to appear more casual than he really was. I glanced at him, wondering suddenly if he were as nervous as I. 'We are off to our bed. We will see you on the morrow, brother.'

I felt a dart of surprise at the familiar term but Cynddylan merely put down his cup, wiped his hands on his leggings and stood up, kissing me on the forehead.

'Good night, little sister.'

I accepted his kiss, fighting back tears, wanting to cling to him like an infant and beg him to break the contract and let me stay home. Damn Pengwern and the incessant war treaties. My shaking hand gripped his forearm, my fingers knotting in the fabric of his sleeve but his own grip tightened, silently reminding me of my duty. There was nothing he could do to save me now but as he drew away I thought I saw in the back of his eyes a sudden flash of pity.

Six

Braziers burned, warming the chamber and extra furs had been placed upon the bed. Cadafael poured me a drink and I gulped it greedily in desperation, wishing I had taken more mead when I had the chance. The indignity that was to come would be easier if I were drunk.

He put down his own cup, strolled toward me and lifted my chin, not quite looking me in the eye. I thought he would kiss me and I stood rigid, swallowed deeply and closed my eyes, waiting for his lips but when I opened them again he had moved away.

He took off his sword and mantle and tossed them into the corner then sat on the bed pulling at his boots. My time with Osian had spoiled me. I had expected poetry and sweet talk but I learned quickly that being bedded by Cadafael would be very different from the gentleness I had known before.

'Come and help me.'

I hesitated for a moment and then, realising he expected me to act as his body-servant, I crossed the room and knelt at his feet. Slowly, my fingers unused to such tasks, I began to fiddle with the thong until at last it was free. As I slid it free, the stench of his unwashed feet hit me and I stood up breathless and placed his stinking boot by the fire.

There would be no seduction.

I stood gazing into the hearth where the flames leapt like tiny orange and yellow sprites performing some fiery ritual, making me want to throw myself in. My heart was beating like a hare's. I wanted to scream at him to get dressed, didn't know where to look as this huge, hairy stranger began to remove his leggings. When he was quite naked, he blew out the candles leaving me to manage as best I could in the light of the brazier. I wanted to call for Gwawr to brush my hair and help me change but thought better of it and wriggled from my tunic to crawl beneath the covers in my kirtle.

That first night as a married woman was by no means pleasant but it was not as bad as I had feared. Cadafael was not Osian and I quickly realised that I had been lucky with my first experience for my husband was not a skilled lover. His hands were cold, his breath rank with mead and there was no delightful kissing, no gentle stroking as there had been with Osian. He fumbled with my shift, wrenching it up to my neck while I shut the memory of Osian away and tried not to weep with humiliation. When he rubbed a large rough skinned hand across my breasts and kneaded my nipples I made no sound and when, to my great astonishment, he rolled me onto my belly and mounted me as if I were one of Cynddylan's bitches, I still made no sound, but bit down hard upon the bed cover and held my breath.

While he sweated above me I stared wide-eyed into the dark and longed for him to finish. It was not love making, not as I had known it, it was just a joining of two bodies for the sake of procreation. He did not hurt either my person or my spirit but when he was done and slipped into snores, I felt so empty and so alone that I lay awake for a long time, watching the dawn creep into the chamber.

In my mind's eye I saw the future stretched before me. Night after night of Cadafael's unskilled, untender attention. I had no illusion that I would ever escape this joining. I could only ever be freed from it should either sickness or childbirth take me and I wasn't really ready for death ... not then.

PART TWO
CADAFAEL'S TUNE

The mountain, were it still higher
I will not covet, there to lead my life.

I did not see Osian again and although my heart ached for him I did not seek him out, not once I was tainted by another's hand. A few days later Ffreur and I rode away from our childhood home for the Kingdom of Gwynedd where Cadafael ruled. Neither of us had left the safe enclosing arms of Pengwern before and although Ffreur's tears were soon dried by the novelty of travel and the surprising sights that unfolded before us, I mourned internally for the length of the journey.

    A light misting rain wet us through as we travelled across the fertile lands of Powys, skirting the higher hills and keeping to the windward side of the valley. When we passed through hamlets, the sound of the horses brought the peasants from their dark hovels to stand at the roadside and watch us pass. Some of them were filthy and ragged, too dogged by life to raise a cheer but the young ones called out, waved their arms above their heads while their elders, overawed at our splendour, watched open mouthed as we passed by. Freur and I rode at the head of the cavalcade while Gwawr, too old to straddle a pony, came behind on the back of a produce cart, her bulk slumped like a big, lumpy sack of flour. When we reined in our mounts to see how she was fairing, she grumbled loudly at the indignity and showed Hild the rough edge of her tongue when the girl dared to snigger at her undignified predicament.

Iestyn constantly returned to his bride's side, ensuring her every comfort and I felt a twang of envy at Ffruer's pleasure in his company. She turned her pink face up to him and allowed him to wipe the rain from it with his kerchief, and when we stopped for noonday rest they tiptoed away from the main party to be on their own. Their mutual affection made me hunger all the more for Osian but each mile we travelled put him further and further from me.

I am sure that Cadafael paid me no thought at all. Things might have been easier between us had he been more attentive so that some sort of relationship might have developed between us but he was curt to the point of rudeness. He kept with the men of his teulu, his hearth troop, discussing the route and the need for more bridges to be built on the mired road between Gwynedd and Pengwern.

My buttocks were red raw from the saddle and my relief was immense when night began to fall and we rested at the home of one of Cadafael's retainers. I looked around the rough roofed hall where children stood, runny nosed in the steady rain and felt homesickness take a deeper bite. But once inside, although I found the accommodation to be poor, the fire was hot and I welcomed the steaming bowl of cawl that was thrust into my hand.

It was a far cry from the luxury I was used to and when I was shown to a makeshift bed in the corner of the hall, I couldn't quite believe that Cadafael truly expected me to share it with him. But at his grunted instruction I slipped from my tunic and climbed on to the mattress and pulled a fur up to my chin. While my husband made use of my body I lay and listened to others coupling not far away, the sounds of their pleasure illustrating quite clearly the delight that I lacked.

In the morning we were not offered privacy in which to wash and dress but with Gwarw's assistance I managed with some dignity. As I cast my sorry gaze about the squalid hall, homesickness bit deeply and it was with some alarm that I realised that life in Gwynedd may not be as gentle as it had been in the famed opulence of Cynddylan's Hall.

With stiff limbs we remounted our ponies and the journey began again, this time in watery sunshine. By noon the sun came out surprisingly warm for a winter's day and I threw off some of my furs to enjoy the warmth on my face and arms. Ffreur trotted up to join me, her hair bouncing prettily on her shoulders.

'What a rough place that was, Heledd. I hope Cadafael's hall will be more comfortable. Iestyn says it is but you can never tell with men, their idea of comfort is very different to ours. I expect we can send to Cynddylan for some essentials though.'

The main essential I lacked was Osian and a soft seat. My backside was so sore I expected never to find comfort again but I smiled and murmured that I was sure the King of Gwynedd's hall would be less spartan than that of his retainers.

It was one of those infuriating days when it is too hot one minute and chilly the next and, quite suddenly the sun was less warm and a glance at the sky showed that small clouds had clustered before it. I called for my cloak and no sooner had I tied the strings beneath my chin that the rain began again, this time in earnest.

It fell steadily, soaking our garments, chilling our bones and, what with my sore buttocks and stiff red fingers, and my aching heart, my misery was complete. The rain wet my face, trickled down my cheeks, mingling with my sorrowful tears. Then my nose began to run and I could not find my kerchief and, consumed with misery, I felt my chin wobble and my chest tighten. It was with no small relief when the horses began to strain up the foothills and Iestyn rode back to tell us we approached the track that led to Cadafael's llys.

Far up in the sky tiny black birds keened and as we craned our heads back to look at them, Iestyn told us they were eagles but we could not see them clearly for swift dark clouds came down again and swathed them in mist. It was a wild and bleak place and it was easy to see we would be at the mercy of the elements living here. I pulled my hood about my face and put my head down for the last upward haul. To my surprise the sturdy horses, used to the sliding shale and dripping vegetation, made easy work of it. I clung to my mount's mane, leaning forward in the saddle and once safely through the gate and in the shelter of the courtyard I slipped thankfully to the ground. Without so much as sparing the time to look about me, I followed the party into the warmth of the royal hall.

Gwawr helped me off with my cloak before pulling off her own and draping them over a chair, complaining loudly as she did so.

'Oh, mercy, mercy. I have been shaken and rattled every step of the way.' She sat down and eased off her boots, wiggling her fat toes before the fire. I joined her on the bench, stretched out my own feet, the flames a welcome luxury after the long ride.

'I thought I would never be warm and dry again.'

Ffreur flopped in a seat beside me, unravelling layers of clothing. She emerged pink and glowing, her large eyes strikingly blue. Looking around the hall, she summoned a passing servant for a drink, already confident and happy in her new position. She would have made Cadafael a far better queen than I.

Servants hurried to bring us refreshments, the fires were stoked and the torches were lit, all at once making the hall more cheerful. A bowl of cawl was thrust into my hand and I began to spoon it into my mouth, the hot liquid warming me from the inside. As I chewed on a succulent piece of mutton I began to feel slightly more cheerful.

Across the hall I saw Cadafael, who had been besieged by his household steward as soon as we arrived, place his hand on the shoulder of a young girl who nodded to the questions that fell thick and fast upon her. I was surprised to see him so concerned with domesticity, almost as much as I was surprised to see how the household seemed genuinely glad of his return. I scanned the hall, assessing its worth and noting any changes that may be necessary.

It was not as rich as Cynddylan's hall. The wall hangings were not so finely woven and the iron fittings were crudely made in comparison. I knew Cadafael was rich, probably richer than my brother but it seemed he lacked his taste for finery. I did not mind the lack for compared with last night's lodging, at least the hall was warm and comfortable. I would soon rectify any defects.

The flames leapt so high in the hearth that I soon began to feel a little too hot and loosened my tunic at the neck. A group of small children ran into the hall, dodging between the trestle tables shouting, a dog in hot pursuit and I looked up, suddenly realising that I had been missing the constant noise of my younger siblings.

'Quiet,' yelled Cadafael, turning a dark countenance upon them but although the children quieted a little, the dog barked all the more. My lips twitched. My husband narrowed his eyes and I laughed aloud, the sound escaping before I could prevent it.

One of the children, taking refuge from his fellows, ran to me and playfully grabbed my skirts, hiding behind my legs. He was laughing, his face red, his hound at his heel beating a tattoo upon my knee with his tail. The boy and his dog ran in a circle round and around me while Cadafael looked on with a thunderous expression.

'Get that child away from the queen,' he yelled and the young servant girl ran forward.

'No, no,' I held out my hand. 'It is quite alright, I love children.' I sat down and, scooping the boy onto my knee, put a hand to the dog's head to quiet it.

'What are you called?' I asked the boy. He was about three, a fat, sturdy child who reminded me of my youngest brother, Gwion. He leaned his head against my breast, his heart beating rapidly beneath my hand.

'Twm,' he said and wiped his nose on his sleeve. His companions watched from the other side of the table.

'Well, Twm,' I said, 'I think it best you all quieten down a little now, it won't do to anger the King on his first evening home.'

A glance at Cadafael told me his temper was cooling. He lifted his chin and made his way across the hall toward us and at his approach the child wriggled under my hands.

'Children suit you, Madam; I look forward to seeing you with offspring of your own.' I flushed and allowed the boy to slide from my knee. Once free, he ran back to the other end of the hall to where his playmates waited.

I wanted children of course, all women did, but the conception of them was something I certainly did not welcome. Cadafael may be tall and handsome but he was an ungentle and selfish lover, although I would never have realised the fact had I not once been loved by a better man.

I suddenly became aware that Cadafael was watching me with an intent expression on his face and when I coldly raised my chin, he turned abruptly and quit the hall, jerking his head to his staff. The servant girl bobbed me a curtsey and followed in his wake.

While I sat and wondered what I should do next Ffreur sighed suddenly beside me. She stretched and yawned, overcome by the heat of the fire. Iestyn snapped his fingers at a hearth wench.

'You, girl, take my wife to my sleeping place and make her comfortable.' As Ffreur rose he pulled her back down briefly onto his lap and I heard him whisper, 'Make yourself comfortable, I will join you shortly.'

Two

My own bower was furnished with all I could require. As queen, I was given private quarters, separate from the King. Flames crackled in a large hearth and many torches burned around the walls and a brazier was pulled close to the bed. I would not want for heat or light. I sat on the bed, dug my fingers into the furs and tested the ropes. It was well strung and the mattress seemed to be deep and soft. While Gwawr bumbled about the chamber putting my things away in chests, my combs and casket of jewels on the dresser, I sat on the edge of the bed and pondered my sorry future. I was bone weary and, feeling over warm after the freshness of the journey, I loosened my tunic and wondered if I would need all the furs that were piled around me.

Beside a richly carved chair lay a small harp. I ran my fingers across the strings, immediately regretting it as the sound evoked the tenderness of Osian, sharpening my loss and bringing stinging tears to my eyes. The sorrow that bit deep into my throat was a pain I had come to know well and I turned away from it, closing my eyes upon the past, trying to blank it out and look to the future, as bleak as it was.

'Gwawr, help me with my tunic, I think I will lie down awhile. I am so tired.' She shuffled toward me and began to loosen my lacings.

'It will be suppertime soon, I should think,' she complained. Gwawr always grumbled if she could but I never paid it any notice for I knew it was merely a habit and not a sign of discontent.

'Then I will miss supper, if I have to.' I flopped miserably onto the bed, sinking into the softness and closed my eyes, wanting to sleep but kept awake by my disobedient mind that insisted on reliving every jolt of the ride.

I thought I should never sleep for the noises of the llys were strange to me but I must have dozed off quite quickly because the next thing I knew, I jumped awake to find Cadafael in the room, tossing a log into the flames.

I raised my head just in time to witness an explosion of sparks that leapt up and smoke billowed into the chamber. I coughed and flopped back down again while he took a large bite of an apple and turned to where I lay.

'Ah, did I wake you? Supper will not be long.' I pulled myself onto the pillows and blinked at him.

'Where is Gwawr?'

'Who?'

'My woman, Gwawr, where is she? I will need her to help me dress.'

He threw the core into the fire and licked the tips of his fingers.

'I sent her away, we have some business first.'

He stood at the foot of the bed and my heart began to race as he moved to sit on the mattress beside me. With two fingers he lifted a strand of my hair from my breast and loosened the neck of my shift. Not now, I thought, wildly, please, not now, not in daylight. But I fought down rising panic, trying to still the rise and fall of my bosom, fearful he may mistake it for passion. When he reached out and began to explore my body, I kept my eyes fixed firmly on his face. I watched his pupils darken, his cheeks become suffused with blood as his ardour increased but his kneading and rubbing did nothing but turn my stomach.

When he pulled my kirtle over my head and tossed it onto the floor, leaving me naked, I turned away from him to crawl beneath the cover but he put out a hand and stopped me. He pushed me back onto the mattress and climbed onto the bed, his breath heavy and his movements clumsy. I closed my eyes trying to pretend that I wasn't really naked in the presence of a strange man in full daylight.

This time the act lasted longer. He seemed more relaxed, more inclined to enjoy and prolong the moment. I lay passive, letting him have his will until at last his grip on me tightened, his voice grew hoarse and his movement quickened. Then I screwed up my face and clenched my muscles hard to make a quicker end to it all.

He slumped down upon me, totally swamping me. He was on top of me, his hair in my face, his torso crushing mine, my nostrils full of his odour, his dwindling ardour still heavy in my quaint. I was trapped, totally and horribly pinioned beneath him while he overwhelmed me, expelling everything that was Heledd and turning me into his possession. His chattel.

When, without a word he got up and wiped himself on my discarded kirtle, I pulled the furs up to my chin and watched as he refastened his leggings and picked up his sword belt. He stood hesitantly before me but still he did not speak. I fastened my miserable eye upon a huge jewelled buckle that glistened just above his groin and waited for him to say something but his words never came. He just turned abruptly and walked away and, when the door closed and his footsteps faded, I rolled over and buried my face into the mattress.

I lay there unmoving until I heard Gwawr's quiet footsteps. I rolled on to my back and stared at the rafters and let hot tears ooze from beneath my eyelids into my ears. She made no comment but, taking a bowl of warm water, came to the bed and began to bathe my private places. Her cloth was warm and soft, soothing the soreness and dulling some of the pain. After a few moments she began to hum and then to sing, and when I recognised the songs that she had sung to comfort me when I was small, my tears began again in earnest.

Three

645 AD

I had everything a woman could ask for; fine clothes, warm bed, good food and a powerful husband yet I was miserable in my marriage. I silently scolded myself, told myself not to waste time mourning for Osian for it was hopeless, I would not see him again. He was gone from me and would never be back but I was desperate for someone to love, something solid to cling to and make life worthwhile, and so I prayed, to both the old gods and the new, to send me a child.

That prayer was swiftly answered and it was just three months later that my courses stopped. When first I spoke of my suspicion to Gwawr, she mopped a tear with the edge of her apron.

'He will leave you be now, child, just for a while until your churching. A man never bothers a wife once she has quickened.' Her words filled me with optimism. I counted on my fingers. I had six months to go and another month before my churching. Seven months without the burden of Cadafael's lust. It was like a gift from the gods.

Just to be free of his clumsy lovemaking I told my husband I had quickened as soon as I could but for the first time ever, Gwarw was wrong. To my great disappointment he kept on coming to my chamber, night after night, until well into the six month. It was my misfortune that his technique did not improve with the practice, and it seemed he had no concept that I could be given pleasure too. He viewed my body solely for his gratification and it was not until my belly became too grotesque to tempt him any longer that mercifully, he stayed away.

'Oh, Heledd, you are lucky.' Ffreur hugged me and then sat back on her haunches, tears in her eyes. She lowered her head. 'Iestyn and I long for a child and yet, for all our effort, there has been nothing.'

'Give it time, child,' Gwawr butted in, putting a tray of cups before us on the table. 'You have always been too impatient. Heledd is just fortunate. You will quicken in time. In the meantime you can help your sister to prepare for her birthing and learn what is in store for you.'

Most days, as my pregnancy progressed, I grew more irritable and hated myself for my bad humour. My back ached, my ankles swelled fatter than Gwawr's and I was forced to make constant trips to the privy. Confined to my chambers, I was bored with my needlework and longed to ride abroad, or stride across the mountain top or climb down to the valley floor. Too often I snapped at Ffreur, feeling a pang of guilt when her face fell at my unkind words.

At nightfall, when Gwawr helped me to bed I looked upon the huge dome of my belly and despaired of ever being normal again. She rubbed salves into my stretched skin, the warm penetrating aroma, providing fleeting comfort. The village wise-woman, Ceri, swore that the concoction would permeate into my womb and ensure my son was both brave and wise.

I was doing my duty, providing the King with an heir and all I could do was rail against the inconvenience while with every passing month, when her courses came with sickening regularity, Ffreur grew more and more despondent.

She sat on my bed watching the outline of my son's foot track across my belly and put out a gentle hand to feel his strong kick. 'He will be a great King like his father,' she said. 'He is vigorous already.'

'Do you think Cadafael is so great a King?' I asked. 'I think he is over-harsh with the people. In times of want a good King should turn a blind eye to small crimes like poaching and theft. How else can a man be expected to keep his family fed in times like these?'

I was becoming opinionated on many things, often moralising on matters I knew nothing about. Ffreur looked a little shocked.

'But to ignore crime is to encourage chaos, suppose everyone stole to keep meat on the table?'

I flung my legs over the side of the bed and strode impatiently up and down the chamber. It seemed to me that a man who had usurped another's kingdom had no place to complain of thieves.

'We have more than enough here in the llys. Look at that table, there is more food here than I will need in a week, yet the common folk are starving and falling sick.'

Ffreur let her hands fall into her lap, her usually bright eyes dark and tragic.

'I wonder why God lets these sad things happen? If he sent enough rain the crops would not fail and the animals would fatten instead of dying, then the people would thrive. There are some that say that mankind has committed a great sin and that we are all paying for it. I pray daily for God to release the poor from famine.'

'I think this new God of yours is no better than the old. There is still war and hunger and suffering for all the priests tell us that He is a benign, forgiving God.' With a glance about the chamber to make sure that my confessor was not near, I drew her closer. 'When I am alone, Ffreur, I pray to the old mother spirits … and there are many who still do.'

Ffreur was pale, she raised her eyes to mine, brought her head close and whispered, 'And do they answer, Heledd?'

I laughed and the sound was bitter even to my own ears. 'I think so. I am after-all with child while you remain barren.'

Her face slackened, her eyes filled. Why did I do it? The pain I caused her offered me no easement. I forced myself to acknowledge the truth. I was envious for she had the man she loved while I was forced to bear the child of a man I loathed. I reached out, full of remorse.

'I am sorry, Ffreur, I didn't mean it. That was thoughtless.'

She kept her face lowered.

'I know, Heledd. I understand that life is hard for you. I would be happy if I could bear a child but you, well, I think you will never be truly content will you, even once your child is here?'

Her eyes were penetrating, I looked away, her words stinging, forcing me to see that I was far from the gentle woman I had always intended to be. Dissatisfaction was making me cruel. But I was spared the need of replying when the door opened and Gwarw waddled in, a slave bearing a tray of mead behind her.

'Put it there,' she pointed to the table and the girl crossed the room, before bobbing a curtsey and turning to leave.

'Wait,' I commanded and the girl stopped, slowly raising her eyes to mine. I had seen her before but she did not usually serve me. There was something different about her to the other slaves, her bearing was proud, although she had no right to be. This was the first time I had seen her up close and I was struck by the clarity of her eyes and her smooth, flawless skin.

'What is your name?'

She licked her lips, cleared her throat. 'Angharad, Lady.'

Usually my servants looked at the floor but this one held my gaze as if she were my equal.

'You do not usually serve me? Where is Hild?'

'She is sick, Lady. I am doing Hild's duties until she recovers.'

I nodded and flicked my fingers toward the door to indicate she should leave. When she had gone, I turned to Gwarw. 'You didn't tell me Hild was sick. I hope she is not contagious.'

Gwarw slopped some wine into a cup and handed it to me.

'She scalded her hand and can barely grip anything but she will be recovered soon enough.'

'That girl, Angharad, she is strange. There is something about her I am not sure I like.'

Gwarw grunted noncommittally and struggled to her feet, insisting that it was time I lay down before supper.

'I envy you the luxury of rest in the afternoon,' she moaned as she removed my slippers and tucked a pillow behind my head. 'Now, get some sleep or there will be no feasting for you this evening.'

'You can rest if you please,' I told her in an effort to be kind but she snorted rudely through her nose as if I were still the five-year-old Heledd and not the Queen of Gwynedd at all.

'I have duties to attend, child, now turn over and close your eyes.' She drew the curtains about the bed, shutting out the day and I shifted my bulk to a comfortable position, crooked my legs and tucked a knuckle into my mouth, as was my habit.

When I awoke the fires had burned down and although I could hear that supper had begun in the hall, the chamber was silent apart from Gwarw's gusty snores. I lumbered from the mattress and poured myself a drink and Gwarw, hearing me moving around, snorted a few times before stirring and clambering from her chair.

'I must have dropped off,' she said, stretching her old limbs and picking up the comb. She wrenched at my tangled hair.

'Ow,' I protested, snatching the comb away and beginning to tease the knots out myself. Gwarw grumbled and began to tidy away my things, folding them anyhow and shutting the lid of the clothes press just a little too sharply. As I left the room to join the feasting, I flashed her a warning look before striding along the corridor, eager to join the throng. Maternity made me ravenous and my mouth sprang alive at the smell of roasting pork. I quickened my step, eager for my dinner, if not the dancing.

The musicians were warming up and I was glad to see that I had not missed supper after all. Unnoticed, I slipped through the door and took my seat beside Cadafael and to my surprise, as Angharad leaned across to fill his cup, I saw him reach out and caress her arse. I froze, my gaze fixed on his roving hand. She did not flinch from his touch and when he withdrew she flicked back her hair and tossed him a bold smile. I was shocked. She was even younger than Ffreur.

Cadafael, noticing me at last, raised his mead cup and I gestured that Angharad should fill my own. Then, still in a sort of stunned daze, I saluted my husband before drinking deeply and looking about the hall with my head high.

Despite a twinge of injured pride I did not really care where my husband's fancies took him, as long as it wasn't toward me but throughout the evening I could not help but notice how Cadafael's eyes followed Angharad about the room. His lust for her was obvious and I wondered if he'd had her yet or if he waited his chance. As I tapped my feet to the music and filled my belly with roasted pork, a strategy began to bubble in the cauldron of my mind.

That evening, just to be sure, I left my bed and waited in the shadows near to Cadafael's chamber. I drew my cloak about me and wriggled my toes to keep them from going numb for the night was cold.

Whether I wanted them to be guilty or not, I could not tell but my belly churned in nervous anticipation as I waited for their footstep. The sounds of drunkenness in the hall began to grow less ribald and the hour grew so late that dawn was a pale stripe in the east but, just as I decided to return to my bower after all, I heard a light footfall and the murmur of voices. I flattened myself against the wall and waited a little longer.

My husband made unsteady progress along the passage, walking with the careful step of a drunkard. His arm was slung about the shoulder of his page, and when the boy threw open his chamber door Cadafael thanked him politely, dropped his cap on the floor and thanked the boy once again when he retrieved it for him. Then, placing a heavy hand on his shoulder he pushed his face too close. I saw the boy pull away from his wine-laced breath.

'I am lonely, Gwidion, my wife doesn't like me. Are you ever lonely?'

I put a hand over my mouth to stifle a giggle, wanting to hear the boy's reply but his voice was muffled as he half carried Cadafael to his bed. As they lit the candles a sliver of light showed beneath the door and as I crept away I could hear Cadafael singing a bawdy song about a priest and a ploughboy.

I was surprised to see him so maudlin, his usual brash confidence fuddled by the mead he had drunk. I thanked the gods that he had never come to my chamber in that state. He was repugnant enough without being totally pickled in mead.

I had just a few hours left in which to sleep and once safely back in my own apartments, I slid between icy sheets. It took a long while before the feeling returned to my toes and, thinking of Ffreur tucked up with her husband in the warmth of their marriage bed, I envied her afresh.

Isolation crowded in on me. I crossed my arms about myself and held on tight but it did nothing to alleviate the loneliness. These days I seldom allowed myself to dwell on him but, as a bitter-sweet treat, I allowed my thoughts to return to Osian. I closed my eyes, remembering his golden smile, his downy soft kiss, his skilled hands, and just for a short while, curled in the centre of my lonely bed, I felt a little warmer.

Four

A few days later Cadafael rode out with the teulu. I watched the dust from the horses' hooves dwindle before I summoned Angharad to my presence. Then, wanting to appear relaxed and in command, I settled myself at the hearth with my needle.

After a while there came a slight scratching at the door and she was there, meekly dipping a greeting, her head bowed. The sight of her in her drab tunic reminded me that she was just a slave and I should not fear her so, assuming a queenly expression, I beckoned her forward. In the corner my attendants craned their necks, eager to know our business but I waved them back to their chores and invited Angharad to join me.

'Sit,' I said and she hesitated only briefly before perching uncertainly on Gwarw's stool. 'Would you hold this for me?' I offered her a skein of wool and she took it, held it taught while I began to wind.

Initially I spoke of trivial things, obtaining monosyllabic responses. It was hard work, making friends with a scullion. I looked at her and wondered how to bridge the gulf between us. She was seated lower than myself as befitted her station and I could see her scalp gleaming white where her hair parted in the centre. The hands that clutched the wool trembled. It was apparent she believed herself to be in some trouble and I felt a sudden rush of guilt. I had taunted her long enough. I decided to be blunt.

'You please me, Angharad,' I said and she looked up, and blinked a few times before she spoke.

'Pleased you, Lady, how have I done that?' Her voice was softly questioning. I sat back and smiled at her smugly,

'By pleasing My Lord King.'

It gave me a twinge of pleasure to see her turn so pale. She swallowed and blinked rapidly, unable to look me in the eye. The ill-will of the queen meant certain torment for a slave and when her trembling visibly increased, I put out a hand and touched her knee, offering friendship but she flinched and ducked her head.

'I don't know what you mean, Madam,' she whispered and my answering laugh rang out merrily, rousing my attendants from their chores. I curtly signalled that they should mind their business.

'Yes, you do, girl. I know he likes you. Have you lain with him yet?'

Her face grew flaccid with fear and, taking pity, I reached out a hand to her again. 'Angharad, it does not displease me. In fact, the prospect delights me and I want to make you a gift.'

I had her attention now. She looked at me as if I were moon-mazed. Like an animal in a trap she did not move, her wide eyes glistened darkly and a small vein pulsed in her neck as she awaited my next words.

Fumbling at my girdle, I drew forth an arm ring. It was not a costly piece, just a trinket crafted by the smiths of Pengwern but, to Angharad, it represented unimaginable wealth. She stood up, spilling the wool onto the floor. 'Madam!' she cried, stepping away from me. 'I cannot take that.'

I grabbed her hand and pulled her back onto the stool.

'Of course you can.' I smoothed her hair, almost crooning, determined to lure her into my pay. 'I want us to be friends.'

Our faces were close, sweat glistened on her skin and great diamond drops hovered on her lashes before over spilling onto her cheek. She was so nervous I could smell the scent of her body, sweet and musky. I pushed the bracelet between her brown fingers. She sniffed and shook her head from side to side. 'I don't understand,' she whimpered.

I leaned toward her.

'Do not cry, child. Just as long as you keep my husband from my bed, I will be your friend and continue to reward you. You must make yourself … irresistible.' I pushed the arm ring over her hand. 'There, isn't that fine?'

The golden band was delicately traced with knots and studded with small gems. I stroked the smooth, golden skin on her arms and turned her hands up in mine. They were work-worn and reddened, the nails broken and …they were the hands of a child. A squirm of guilt stirred in my belly. It was wicked to tempt innocence into whoredom but I pushed the thought away and smiled a blithe smile. The girl was a slave, fated to live miserably and die young, so what difference would it make to her. By alleviating her poverty I was doing her a favour.

'I look forward to seeing you again soon, Angharad. You may go now. You know what you have to do. I will be watching.'

Her mouth worked as she sought the correct words but in the end she could not find the right thing to say. She turned away, pulling her sleeve over the arm ring to conceal it and left the chamber with her head bowed. I sat back in my chair, and watched her go, biting my lip and hoping I had done right.

Five

Shortly after that, as I had hoped, Cadafael's visits to my chamber decreased. A few nights later, I waited again in the passage near his chamber. This time I had taken the precaution of wrapping a warm fur about me and burying my feet in thick boots. The llys was quiet, only the gentle rumblings of a community settling for the night. A dog barked and I heard someone yell at it to quiet then, as peace settled again, I tucked my hands beneath my armpits and waited.

At length, two shadowy figures came, arms linked, along the corridor. They made little sound but I could tell by the way my husband leaned heavily on his companion that he was drunk again. He had never come to my bed drunk and I wondered whether he intentionally remained sober when he planned to spend the night with me. The door was thrown open, the torches within illuminating the features, not of his page this time, but of Angharad.

I smiled grimly at my victory.

As the portal closed behind them, I stood very still and heard Cadafael give a sudden shout of laughter and her answering giggle ... then silence. I strained my ears but after a few moments I realised that I was eavesdropping and, rather shocked at the tiny squirm of envy, I tiptoed back to my lonely chamber.

The room was in deep shadow, the only light issuing from the banked up fire. Gwawr had turned back the bed covers in readiness but had given up waiting and now snored loudly in her closet. I did not wake her but after taking a draught of mead, pulled off my own boots and climbed into bed.

For a long time I lay sleepless, trying not to imagine Angharad's pubescent body debauched by Cadafael's, his heavy bearded mouth bruising her plump lips. It was a picture I did not like and I discovered that I did not relish my part in it. For the first time self-hatred rivalled the contempt I bore my husband.

Tortured by remorse and haunted by the possible consequences, I tossed and turned into the small hours but by the time dawn had begun to pink the night sky I had convinced myself that I acted for the good of my unborn child and I turned over and drifted into a heavy sleep.

Six

In the long months that followed I strayed further and further from the woman my mother had raised me to be. As a girl I had imagined myself married to some great prince, I would make a compassionate queen, giving succour to the needy and comfort to the suffering. Instead, as my bad temper grew as rapidly as my belly, I barely left my apartments and made myself a burden to both Ffreur and my serving women. Nothing pleased me, my food tasted of ashes, my thirst was unquenchable and the longing in my heart for Osian grated at the edges of my sanity.

To her credit Ffreur tried to distract me. She buried her envy at my condition and sat beside me, spinning yarn or plying her needle to produce tiny garments for the expected prince. She spoke of small things, memories of our childhood at Pengwern, reminiscing about our mother and the birth of our many siblings.

'Mother brought forth all her children with such ease, Heledd, you are sure to do the same.'

Her head was bent over her work, she was straining her eyes in the poor light, anxious to finish the garment she was working before I was brought to bed.

'Much good it did her,' I retorted nastily. 'She survived multiple childbirth to perish of the fever. It might have been as well as to have died bearing Cynddylan and been spared all the subsequent pain.'

'Heledd!' Ffreur was so effortlessly shocked, her mild sensibilities so easily bruised. I gave a short laugh, a sound that was bitter even to my own ears.

'What? Can you not imagine the world without us? Do you think we are here for a purpose or that we make any difference? Nothing we do or say will have the slightest impact on the world or those in it.'

'We are all part of God's plan...' she began but stopped and looked at me sorrowfully when I gave a loud derisive snort.

'If this life is the result of any sort of plan, then your God must be a cruel entity indeed.' Her face pinched with distress, Ffreur sighed and put down her sewing to come and crouch at my knee. Her hands were cold, the tips of her fingers reddened by the needle.

'Is it so bad, Heledd? You are soon to have a child; your husband is a rich and powerful King, your life comfortable. What more could a girl ask?'

Osian's face swam in my mind's eye and I felt again the gentle caress of his hands, the softness of his lips. I longed for him so much but I swallowed against the surging sorrow and placed my hands on my swollen belly.

'I am just so uncomfortable. No matter how I sit, or where I lie, my back feels as if it is broken in two and look, Ffreur, look at my ankles. Would you want ankles like that?'

She looked at them and, shifting her position, took my left foot on to her lap, pushed off my slipper and began to rub my feet, massaging my toes, bending my ankles and rubbing the aching joint.

'I would gladly have ankles like this if it meant I were soon to bear my husband a child. I would suffer any indignity or pain just to see the joy on Iestyn's face when he beheld our firstborn.'

I lay my head back, shamed by her honesty, diminished by her acceptance.

'I am sorry, Ffreur. Sorry to be so thoughtless of your own cares. I will try not to complain any more but will look to you and try to remind myself that my position could be worse.'

It was a vow that I did not keep.

My screams brought Gwawr and Ffreur running. I crouched over a chamber pot and bent double over another, my belly in knots.

'Gwawr!' I cried, tears spouting. 'Help me.' The concern on my old nurse's face was touching. I held out a hand and she grasped it while Ffreur hopped from one foot to the other in the doorway, her brow furrowed.

'Now, now, don't take on so. It's just the babe telling us he will soon be here.'

'The babe?' I gasped. 'No, Gwawr, it is something I've eaten, I've been poisoned!' I leaned over and let loose a stream of vomit and wiped my mouth on the sleeve of my gown. 'You see? Poisoned!'

Gwarw laughed gently and handed me a cup. 'There, rinse your mouth and get to the bed. I want to feel your belly.'

Throwing the cup down, I glared at her.

'It's not the child, I tell you. Ffreur fetch Cadafael, he must be told that someone has tried to harm his queen.' I struggled up from the pot and pulled down my shift. 'If I die, Gwarw, I swear I will take you with me.'

Unmoved at my venom she held my arm and helped me climb onto the bed where I cast myself like a great whale onto the mattress.

Her hands were cold. Her fingers probed my rigid stomach, pressing down hard at the top of my pelvis, making me want to piss.

'Ow!'

She ignored me and gently prised my knees apart. I jumped and swore when she inserted two fingers and pressed down on my belly with the other hand.

'It's the babe alright, the gates are opening.' She wiped her hands on her apron. 'Ffreur poke that girl awake and tell her to get some water on the fire.'

At Ffreur's insistence the servant girl, Hild, her hand quite healed, scrambled to her feet and, although only half awake, began to poke the fire into life.

I sat bad temperedly on the edge of the bed as another wave of pain began to creep across my loins.

'I need to shit again, Gwarw.' I groped for the pot, yanked up my kirtle and sat straining for a while but nothing came. Eventually the cramps subsided and I crawled back to bed. 'What is wrong with me?' I wailed. 'Why am I so sick?'

My head lay in Ffreur's lap and I was calmed momentarily as she stroked back my hair.

'If I should die, Ffreur, get a message to Cynddylan and Cynwraith, tell them that I love them.'

She murmured an assent and continued to soothe me with her gentle hands while great hot tears rolled from my eyes.

'If Gwarw says it is the babe coming, I am sure it must be. After all, she loves you too well to ignore your imminent death.'

They were mocking me, ignoring the danger. Was it not their queen who lay at the brink of eternity while they laughed? I jerked my head from my sister's hands. Nobody understood.

'Don't mock me, Ffreur,' I warned. 'I am about to die, you will never....'

Another pain gripped me, followed quickly by a bout of nausea. I leaned over the bed and vomited into the rushes, my stomach turning inside out. I heaved for a miserable while and after spitting a few times more, sat up, sweating.

'Oh, Ffreur,' I sobbed. 'If I am to die, I hope it's soon. I cannot stand this.'

'Here, drink up.'

I hauled myself up and took the cup that Gwawr was holding, sniffed it, the vile stench almost turning my stomach anew. I held the cup away from me, turned my head.

'What is it?'

'I sent to Ceri for it, she says it will soothe your stomach and ease your labours. She promises if the child does not come easy, she will be here just as soon as she may.'

Ceri was the village wise woman who dwelt at the edge of the forest, sometimes acting as midwife to the mothers of the settlement. I sniffed the potion again.

'It smells worse than the midden.'

'Just drink it.' Gwawr tipped the bottom of the cup and the liquid burned my lips and warmed my tongue before hitting the base of my belly. It was not as bad as I had imagined and after another swig or two my head began to clear and my stomach stopped churning. I said a foul word and gestured for a cup of mead to dispel the taste.

As the potion worked its magic the sickness and flux ceased and the pain was dulled sufficiently to allow me some control. Soon the spasms came regular and strong enough to force me to admit that Gwawr was right. My child was indeed coming.

They built up the fire so high that I could scarcely breathe. Ffreur tied back my hair and I cast off my clothes to squat naked on a blanket on the floor. It was more comfortable so, with the weight of the child off my spine and I crouched there, breathing deeply, trying to summon further strength.

Ffreur, white faced at my agony, clung to my hand and even at the height of my suffering when I threw her off and cursed her for a hindrance, she sought it again as soon as I was quiet. For hours I laboured in the grip of unimaginable torment. I cursed my friends, swore at my servants and cast off every element of my mother's teaching.

Hild brought warm cloths to place upon my belly. They soothed for a while but each time my womb tightened afresh, I threw them off, fighting against the pain, flaying about me with my arms and legs. In the midst of a spasm I caught Gwawr under the chin with my fist. I heard her teeth smash together and Ffreur gasp before she released my hand to help the old woman. But I did not care, I had lost control.

A voice cut through my agony.

'Are you an animal? Sit up and act like the queen that you are.'

I blinked and pushed limp, damp hair back from my forehead. It was Ceri, crawled from her hovel in the wood to tend me. She turned her piercing eyes on my women.

'Get away from her you two. She is undeserving of your care. You girl, get something to staunch the old woman's blood.'

As Hild scurried off to do her bidding, she came to squat beside me and Ffreur and Gwawr backed away. She spoke to me quietly but with such authority that I had to obey. Had I not been in such straights I would have reminded her which of us was queen.

'Now, listen to me, girl, and stop being so foolish. You cannot fight this pain; it always wins. You must harness it, embrace it or it will not release your bairn and he will die, trapped inside the womb and take you with him. Breathe with me, child. Breathe in…breathe out…'

Through a fog of unreality, I watched her draw large blue circles on my belly. I did not understand her magic but as she traced the marks with a bony finger, singing all the while, I felt I was floating and my mind detached itself a little from agonising reality.

I found my chest rising and falling in unison with hers, felt her gnarled old hands on my flesh, her crooked fingers intimately exploring. I caught my breath and she pierced me with her eye again.

'Breathe in … breathe out…'

I did as she bid and found it impossible to remain tense when I breathed that way. I felt her fingers poking and prodding and then, a sickening jolt. She stood up, the stench of her petticoat swamping me. 'There,' she soothed. 'He will come now.'

Ceri held out both hands. 'Come, you must kneel, hands and knees is the best way.'

I followed her instruction and she became my lifeline. Her hands on my bare rump encouraging me to gyrate my hips, she hummed a tune and moved her own body with mine so that it became like a grotesque, sensuous act.

After a while Ffreur crept into the ring of firelight and began to join the humming and I was aware of Gwawr and Hild singing gently as they brought bowls of water and cloths to wrap the babe in.

My child's arrival was imminent.

The pain grew until I felt it had always been a part of me. I was trapped in agony, a purgatory of pain. I thought it would never end but Ceri was inside my mind, directing my thoughts and manipulating my body and so, I somehow knew it would be all right.

The intensity grew. I felt a huge obstruction as if I needed to shit … had to shit.

'Push, my pretty,' Ceri murmured like a lover and I obeyed, pushing down into my bowel to shit my baby out. I felt her hands on my belly, rubbing and pushing. I was no longer a princess or even a queen. I was an animal fighting for my life, fighting to give life to my child.

Ffreur was before me, holding me upright, her breath coming in short gasps as if she were the one in pain. A terrible burning, I forced the thing along the birth canal, felt my skin stretching, tearing. I could not scream, could barely breathe. I panted, eyes wide, kneeling upright in the firelight surrounded by my women.

'That's it, pant a while, wait and then push with the pain when it comes again.' Ceri kept up her crooning as she stroked my belly. I maintained eye contact with Ffreur, concentrating hard on the job I had to do. She did not know it but, had she blinked or looked away, I would have been lost. I could not do it without her.

And then the pain swamped me again. I opened my mouth, spread my legs, released my bowels and pushed like a beast in the field. The child inched reluctantly along the birth passage, with each cramp creeping slowly until I became aware of something lodged between my legs.

I put down a hand to touch wet, steaming hair, a head pulsing with life. MY SON! And with a cry like wild wolves at midnight, I pushed again and he slithered from my body into Gwarw's waiting hands. I flopped onto my back and lay my head in Ceri's stinking lap.

'Heledd. Oh, Heledd.' Ffreur was crying, her face alight with joy. 'It is a boy. You have birthed a beautiful little prince.'

She held him out to me, her face wet and I saw the empurpled, enraged face of my son, his body smeared in birth wax, the purple umbilical cord throbbing and his tiny prick pointing heavenward like a declaration of war.

Seven

Cadafael burst unannounced into the chamber and loomed over the bed. The child was tugging at my breast like a small beast. He looked down at us.

'So, this is my son?' My husband leaned over, his face proud. 'You have done well, wife.'

I acknowledged his words with a slight movement of my head. 'Do you have a preference for a name?'

Cadafael perched on the coverlet. 'Cynfeddw,' he said, as if he had given it much thought. 'After my father. He was a strong man, just as I would want my son to be.'

'Well, I have no preference, so Cynfeddw it shall be. He is as lusty as a piglet, Lord. We must find a wet nurse right away.'

'As you wish,' he said, picking up the tiny fist and balancing it on his finger. 'That is your concern. I will call in to see you both on the morrow.'

He left, leaving me in peace to rest. I closed my eyes, regretting that it was not Osian I had just presented with a son instead of a man I still barely knew.

I left it to Gwarw to find the child a nurse and she chose a young girl from the village whose new born had perished three days after his birth. I gave no thought to the fact that she might be suffering anguish for her loss and merely saw her as a quiet, biddable girl with a plentiful supply of nourishment. After she joined my household I only saw Cynfeddw at intervals during the day and as he continued to grow and thrive, I returned to my former duties. During daylight hours I went about my queenly duties, running the household and overseeing my women but, during the night, I escaped reality and dreamed of Osian, glad for once that he could not see me with my thickened waist and great matronly breasts.

Cadafael on the other hand, made much of his tywysog, his little prince, and visited him every day. Often he sent the nurse away and carried him with him into council to show him off, making himself womanish in his doting. The other lords gathered around, offering parental advice and remarking on the sturdy grip of their new prince.

Cradled in his father's arms the child slept soundly, the ceremonial feathers of the King's cloak tickling his nose as they held council above a sleeping babe. I wondered if the words of the warlords entered his dreams, teaching him the ways of a warrior as he slumbered. Secretly I smiled at the womanish ways of these strident soldiers and the ease with which they were gentled by the presence of a child.

At this time I was reasonably content. Cadafael did not come to my chamber. He was courteous when we met but asked no more of me. For that I was grateful and showered Angharad with trinkets and coin. The girl and I were tentative friends although when we met, we greeted each other coolly as befits a servant and a queen. I never asked if she relished or hated Cadafael's attentions and it mattered little to me then. It was a job of work and I assumed she did it well.

Everyone at the llys knew her for his concubine now. There was no disgrace but I could have wished Cadafael had more concept of discretion. When he beckoned her from her duties to his chamber, although her face burned, she followed him with her head high. Sometimes I pictured him doing to her the things I had suffered and I pitied her, but I quickly learned to push the guilt away and think of other matters. The arrangement worked well until the seventh month after Cynfeddw's birth.

I summoned Angharad to my chamber while the King was absent, ridden forth with my brothers to forge an alliance with the Mercian King, Penda. My sewing women were working on a new tunic for me, richly encrusting the hem and cuffs with precious stones. Clothes were one of my few remaining pleasures and this garment promised to be beautiful and I could not wait to wear it.

I recognised Angharad's hesitant scratching on the door and put down my needle as Gwarw hurried to show her in. She looked peaked and tired, the tip of her nose red as if she had been weeping. My heart gave a little leap of fear.

'What is the matter, have you displeased him?'

She sniffed and shook her head. 'No, Lady, all is well between me and the king. I am ailing, that is all.'

I put a hand to my pocket and drew out a small bag of coin. 'This will make you better. The King will be back in a day or two so ensure you get some rest in the meantime, you are relieved of duty until then. He will want you fresh when he returns, not maudlin and ill.'

I turned to Gwarw who sat in her corner. 'Where are those gowns Ffreur has outgrown, give them to the girl, she can deck herself in those. It might take the king's mind from her dismal expression.'

Gwarw came grumbling and handed Angharad the sack.

'You can go now.' I waved her away with my hand and she made to leave but then hesitated, turned and launched herself at my knee, sobbing. I threw up my hands, alarmed at such a show of emotion while Gwarw groped at her arm and tried to pull her to her feet. 'What is it?' I snapped. 'What are you weeping for?'

'Oh, Lady.' Her face was tragic, tears diluting her dark eyes. She put her hands to her face, her hair falling forward like a curtain. I watched her back heave for a while before my impatience over-spilled. 'Well?'

I looked down upon her, my arms folded, fighting to contain my annoyance. It took her some time to control her tears and speak.

'I carry the King's child.' She sobbed so hard that I could barely hear her words but I understood and a cold, dark fear crept into my stomach and lay there like a sickness.

It was a feeling that did not lift. I had been a fool not to try to prevent this and for the next few months as I watched the slow swelling of Angharad's belly, dreading to see her face bloat and her ankles puff up, I knew that soon I must face my husband's return to my bed.

My own body had long since resumed its shape. My belly was flat again and my ankles trim. Only my breasts remained larger, the nipples brown now instead of pink. They swung gently as I walked, brushing pleasantly against my tunic. In the depths of the night I squeezed them softly and let my thoughts stray to Osian and the way it had been with us, but the thought of resuming intimacy with Cadafael filled me with loathing.

By August Angharad's belly strained at her clothing and she rolled rather than walked as she carried out her tasks. As her bulk increased she was in Cadafael's company less and less and I knew the day would come when he would decide it was time for me to resume my wifely duty. I looked in vain for a likely replacement for Angharad but Cadafael had exclusive tastes and there were none at the llys fair or young enough to tempt him.

Eight

I bumped into Cadafael on his way to the stable one morning. It was a fine bright day and I had been tempted from my bower by the sunshine. Cadafael and I had not met for days. He stopped when he saw me and gestured his companions to go on without him. 'I will catch you up,' he called after them and turned back to me, his hand on his sword hilt, his bearskin cloak moving a little in the wind, the scent of him wafting toward me, stirring intimate memories that I would rather have forgotten.

I blinked calmly into his eyes although the dull thudding of my heart was making me nauseous.

He bowed slightly. 'Madam? I trust you are well.'

I dipped my head, saw his eyes come to rest briefly upon my breasts that were fuller, more matronly now. He smiled; a boyish grin that would have been attractive in any other man. 'I have missed you, wife.' He placed a hand upon my shoulder and compelled me to walk with him. My head was level with his as we strolled to the edge of the settlement and looked down upon the snaking river to where the skerries bobbed against the jetty. Men were loading and unloading supplies brought by boat from afar and we watched them for a while without interest.

His hand slid from my shoulder and came to rest on the small of my back where he let it remain. The smell of horse leather and mead wafted across me again, reminding me of Cynddylan who also loved the hunt. He cleared his throat and I turned to look at him but I did not smile or pretend pleasure in his company. Our gaze held, both of us wary of the other. His face was that of a warrior, his black hair blew across his eyes and his dark beard was untamed. It was a strong face and an open one. In fact, he was a handsome man and, not for the first time, I wondered why I could not love him.

'Come on, Cadafael,' Iestyn called from the stables. 'The boar won't wait.' Cadafael leaned forward and left a kiss on my cheek, flushing like an adolescent.

'I will look in on our son later, Madam and share a cup of mead with you.' And with a swirl of his cloak he was gone. I watched his upright figure hurry across the enclosure and bit my lip, searching for a way out.

I had not visited Ceri's hut before but I knew where it was and, borrowing Gwarw's cloak, I pulled the hood high over my head and shuffled across the settlement. I hoped that if I stooped and pretended to be lame any who saw me would take me for an old woman.

The foot-worn path snaked downhill to where the woods clustered in the valley. My feet slipped on the mud and moisture seeped into my slippers and between my toes. It was a passage forged by years of secret nocturnal visits by the women of the llys. Some said that Ceri had once entertained the young men of the settlement but when her youth and looks faded she began to care instead for the health of the women. They came to her for cures for moon-time cramps, for love potions or to be rid of unwanted brats. Women like Ceri were a boon to any settlement.

I had consulted her several times on trivial things since the birth of Cynfeddw but tonight my need was far from trivial and I was unsure if she could, or would help me at all, for my request was tantamount to treason.

A cat arched its back and spat at me from the windowsill, the inside of its mouth shining pink against the darkness of its coat. I hissed back and it jumped down, disappearing swiftly into the trees as I scratched at the door.

There came a shuffling from within and the wooden portal creaked open. Ceri showed me her gums, her wrinkles deepening as she smiled her welcome.

'Come in, my queen, take a seat by my fire.'

I looked about me, shooed a roosting chicken from a stool and perched before the smoky hearth. There was not enough light to see her face clearly as she shuffled across the room to sit opposite me, the stench of her petticoats making me turn my face away.

'How is the young fellow, does he thrive?'

I nodded. 'Yes, yes, he thrives. I have much to thank you for.'

She grinned in agreement. 'And the other child, your husband's bait, does her belly swell?'

I wondered how she knew. Perhaps Angharad herself visited the old woman. I cursed myself for not having had the foresight to ask for a brew to prevent her pregnancy. I knew such acts were a terrible sin, worse even than the one I planned now and I crossed myself at the thought.

Ceri made a violent sign.

'I'll have none of that in here, not in my own home,' she glared at me. 'Queen or no Queen. It wasn't this new god that got your child out safe was it?'

She held out a cup and I drank from it absentmindedly, the liquid hitting the back of my throat, making tears spring to my eyes. I coughed, spluttered and handed back the cup and she took it from me, cackling with laughter. Then she leaned forward into the firelight and I saw the yellowed wisdom of her eyes, the stringy grey hair lank with grease and crawling things. Could I trust her?

'Of course you can trust me,' she said, although I had not spoken. 'I saved your life and that of your babe, didn't I? And will do again, should you ask it.'

Suddenly making up my mind I grabbed her hand and drew her close, too close for comfort for she stank like a midden.

'I do need help, Ceri, but you must speak of it to no one or it could mean death for both of us.'

She looked down her nose.

'I risk death every day; it holds no fear for me. Now, what is it that you want?'

I licked my lips and quickly made my request before I could change my mind.

Nine

It was full dark when he came to me. I had sent Gwarw to bed and dismissed my women so that I was quite alone. He opened the door without knocking and pretending surprise, I swung my legs from the bed and moved toward him.

'Husband,' my voice was like honey. 'I had all but given you up.'

He swept his eyes up and down my body, taking in the gossamer cloth of my nightgown, my free flowing hair. I looked like a wanton and could almost see his pulse quicken, his ardour rising. He removed his sword belt and threw it in the corner. 'I will pour some mead,' I said and turned away, watching from the corner of my eye as he took a seat on the cushions close to the hearth.

Knowing that my breasts were clearly visible through the thin stuff of my gown, I moved into the firelight and stood before him, handing him his drink. Then I knelt beside him and raised my cup to my lips, smiled over the rim like a harlot before tipping back my head and draining my cup. He did the same, pulled me toward him, entwining his fingers in my hair and I closed my eyes, maintained my smile and emitted a small, convincing groan when he began to nuzzle my neck.

For a while we lay sprawled by the fire. I let him knead my breasts and returned his kisses like a wanton but he did not move me. His beard was rough against my skin and his fingers pinched, his teeth sharp.

'Come,' he said, his voice hoarse. He dragged me to my feet and led me to the bed. 'Get that gown off.'

He began to fumble with his lacings, his breath coming fast while I slid from my kirtle and climbed onto the mattress. When he was naked, my courage flagged a little and I began to fear that Ceri would fail me but, knowing I could not retreat now, I spread myself upon the bed.

'Oh, do hurry, Cadafael,' I whispered and ran a hand across my own body as if I was impatient for him. Thus encouraged, he straddled me, his broad, hairy chest glistening in the torch light and when he began to stroke me again, grunting at the fullness of my breasts, lingering on the softness of my thigh, I wriggled my hips as if I could not wait. To add a little more drama I let out a small squeak. 'Cadafael, I want you…' I lied and opened my eyes full upon him.

His face was suffused with blood, his furred chest heaving. Our eyes locked and then I slowly let my gaze slide down his body to his prick.

'Oh no, Husband,' I cried, in mock dismay. 'Do I not please you?'

He looked down at himself and back at me, appalled to find his cock as wrinkled and as innocuous as a worm. I bit my lip, trying desperately not to laugh and reached out to poke it with my fore finger.

It did not stir.

'You are not quite ready, perhaps?' I remarked and he turned away, rubbing himself frantically for a few moments. Then, staring down at his limp disappointment, he gradually realised that it could not be roused at all and with a look of fury, grabbed his clothes and quit the room, slamming the door hard. I rolled onto my belly, stuffing a pillow in my mouth to curb my laughter. 'Oh, may the gods bless you, Ceri.'

Her potion served me well. Each time Cadafael made an attempt to get a child on me, I added a little powder to his cup and soon, unable to face the humiliation, he stopped coming to my chamber at all. I looked upon it as a victory.

'It only happens with you,' Cadafael sulked on the last time he visited me. 'I don't understand; it's as if I have been bewitched.' Ignoring the sudden chill that his words imparted, I patted his arm.

'Don't worry, Husband, perhaps in time things will come right for us again.'

Looking back now, I can see how cruel it was to weaken the virility of a man like Cadafael but I was young and impetuous. Often, during the course of my day, the memory of his humiliation returned, making me smile and when next I visited Ceri she drew me closer and whispered. 'I had a visit from your man.'

She was consumed by cackling laughter, displaying her pink gums, her cheeks creased with mirth. I couldn't help but smile widely as I waited for her to gain control. 'He untied his leggings, showed me his flaccid member and begged me for a remedy. He assured me it only happens when he is with you.'

She hung onto my sleeve, her body folded as laughter consumed her again. 'I gave him a charm of rat entrails to wear around his neck and suggested that if he didn't fancy you, he should look elsewhere for satisfaction.'

Ceri was a woman after my own heart and by the time Angharad had produced a tiny daughter and resumed her duties as his whore, Cadafael's visits had declined to almost nil. I was glad of that and at the time never dreamed that one day I would seek him out with the sole purpose of seducing him back into our marriage bed.

PART THREE
THE DRUMS OF WAR

Cynddylan, hungry boar, ravager,
Lion, wolf fast holding of descent,
The wild boar will not give back the town of his father.

<u>647 AD</u>

The children toddled ahead toward the river, their cries floating back to us on the wind. At three years old Cynfeddw could already outrun his stout nurse. He looked back over his shoulder, his mouth stretched in laughter as she lumbered after him. Just behind came Angharad's daughter, Medwyl, who imitated everything her half-brother did. Although my son was dressed in finery as befits a prince and Medwyl's drab colours branded her as a servant, their black heads bobbing along in the windblown grass, marked them as siblings.

They were inseparable. Cynfeddw watched over her, fighting her battles as if they were his own, and sharing his friends. I tolerated her presence because it meant my son was happy and left me in peace. He was growing so much like his father, grabbing at what he wanted, demanding obedience and hitting out at those that displeased him. Medwyl was the only person, save his father, who found favour with him.

The nurse caught up, grabbed his arm and bent him over her knee and slapped his arse. My son's face was red with indignation. He rubbed his buttocks and scowled, the image of his father. I stifled a smile at his righteous anger.

It was a fine day, the cloud was high and a brisk breeze blew across the marsh, tossing the birds across the sky. The river that wound its way through the valley brought riches from far afield and we made our way to where a boat was unloading at the jetty. A stream of men, their backs bent beneath the weight of sacks and barrels, unburdened themselves, loading the carts that waited to bear the produce to the llys.

Great preparation was underway for a state visit from my brothers and King Penda of Mercia, and the whole settlement was in an uproar of excitement. There would be feasting and tournaments, a welcome interlude to daily toil. Cynfeddw ran into the crowd and tried to lift one of the heavy sacks, his face turning pink with exertion.

'You can't lift that, come away,' I ordered and Ffreur ran forward to tempt him away with promises of grasshoppers in the meadow. We moved on, they walked before me, hand in hand, Ffreur's fair head bowed to his dark one.

She doted on my son and on Medwyl also, and grieved each month when her own child failed to appear. As the years passed without issue she grew more and more pious, spending long hours on her knees in the cold, stone chapel, doing penance and asking God's blessing. Had I been in her position I would have long since abandoned a God who for so long ignored my prayers but nothing would shake her faith.

I tried to persuade her to visit Ceri, to ask her for a fertility charm but she refused, her face pinched with disapproval. The last years had gone well with me. Cadafael continued to keep away and I felt that having done my duty and produced him with a son, my time was now my own. I had matured well, my body was upright and firm, my teeth still good and my hair fell thick to my waist. I enjoyed my duties as queen, ruling the household, balancing the economy. By day my life was all it should be and I was well content but after dark, when I lay in my lonely bed, although I could barely recall his face, my memory was filled with Osian's lamenting song.

The meadow grasses were indeed rich with grasshoppers and butterflies. The children darted about, squealing every time they caught one to imprison it in their sack. Many people were afraid of butterflies, believing that they were, in truth, witches that crept into the dairy late at night to steal milk and sample the cheese but I laughed at such superstition.

Ffreur followed the children into the long grass whilst I, feeling lazy, sank into the shade of a tree to think my own thoughts. Gwarw busied herself collecting lynden leaves that ward off the coughs and colds of winter and as I watched her, I grew drowsier.

Perhaps it was the tree's affinity with the goddess Venus, whom the Romans had favoured, that made me dream I was with Osian. I saw him clearly, his golden hair, his clear blue eyes. He put down his harp and I ran to him, wept hot tears as I stroked his beard, felt his lips hot upon my neck again. So real was the dream and so filled was it with happiness that I was reluctant to wake and tried to ignore Gwarw and Ffreur calling me back to consciousness.

Eventually, when I could ignore them no more, I sat up and rubbed my eyes. My women were gathered about me, regarding me oddly. Ffreur held the children by the hand and Cynfeddw sucked his thumb, a dark frown upon his face.

'Are you alright, Lady?' Gwarw asked. My tunic had ridden above my knees and I pulled it down, raised a haughty eyebrow and held out a hand to be helped to my feet.

'Of course, why shouldn't I be?'

'You were mumbling and fidgeting in your sleep like a lunatic. Were you having a nightmare, in the daytime? I didn't know if we should wake you or not.' I yawned and looked about me, shivered a little in the breeze.

'I must have been dreaming but I can't recall it.' I realised I had been asleep for some time for the blue sky had been replaced by cloud and the surface of the water was choppy, the skerries bouncing and bumping against the jetty.

It was time to return to the llys if we didn't want to risk a soaking.

We had climbed but half way up the hill when large drops began to fall, making dark splodges on the fabric of my tunic. The hem of my cloak dangled in the mire and in no time our feet were wet through.

Cynfeddw dragged at Ffreur's hand, his plaintive voice complaining while Medwyl, balanced on her nurse's hip, opened her mouth wide and bawled. My own thoughts lingered longingly on my dream and, unheeding of the wet grass and puddles, I kept my head down, enthralled with my private thoughts. At the gate I almost ran into Angharad and she fell into step beside me.

'Your brothers are close now, Lady,' she said, 'a messenger brought word that they are but two hours away.' I put my hand on her shoulder and rested a moment, puffing a little from the climb.

'Good.' I smiled at her and she showed her row of straight teeth in return. 'There will be feasting tonight. I have an old tunic if you'd like it. Come to me before supper and I will look it out for you.'

She flushed and her smile grew wider. 'Thank you, Lady. I will be there.'

'Wait,' I said and kept my hand on her, 'walk with me a little.' She accompanied me through the throng, past the goat pens and the smithy. When we reached the door of my bower I stopped and whispered, 'You are still taking the powders?'

Her eyes were wide as she nodded earnestly. 'Oh, yes, Lady, every morning, as Ceri instructed'

'Good,' I said, 'good girl,' and passed before her beneath the lintel into the warmth of my chambers.

Two

I dressed with special care that evening. I knew my brothers had arrived and would be closeted with Cadafael and Penda in talk of war. I had heard many tales of the Mercian King who was a formidable man and one that my husband and brothers sought to impress. I dressed accordingly, donning my finest tunic and richest jewels. Gwarw was still fussing with my hem as I strode along the corridor toward the hall. Even at a distance the noise was considerable and when the wooden doors, each as thick as a war-hammer shaft, were thrown back to admit me, the din and the heat hit me like a wall.

Every man, woman and child was crammed into the hall space. The central fire roared and the aroma of roasting meat and mead mixed appetisingly in the air. My husband and brothers sat at the top table and I knew the large stranger with them must be Penda.

To my chagrin, my approach went largely unnoticed for all eyes were taken by the antics of my son whom Cadafael had stood on the table while the boy showed off his sword skills to the visiting Kings. I paused half way down the hall, my skin prickling as it warmed in the heat of the fire. I raised my chin, knowing the firelight set my gold jewellery ablaze, and tossed back my thick braids and waited to be noticed.

It did not take very long.

'Heledd!' Cynddylan cried, and leapt over the table to envelop me in his arms. He had quite spoiled my dignified entrance but I smiled upon him and returned his kisses gladly. Cynwraith was next with a gentler greeting that was no less sincere. He squeezed me to him and left a kiss upon my hair.

He had filled out since I had seen him last, his beard grew thicker on his chin and he had himself a bride.

Cadafael rose and as he did so, I noticed Angharad seated a little to his rear, clad in my discarded tunic. I felt a stab of annoyance at his lack of majesty. His whore should be kept for his bedchamber. He held out a hand and turned to his company.

'My queen, Heledd of Pengwern. This is King Penda, of Mercia.'

So, this was the warrior pagan King. The gossips said he was a lover of both war and women and from the looks of him, he carried the scars of both. He was approaching forty, his dark eyes piercing, his mouth sensuous, a scar running from the corner of his eye to disappear into his beard. He was by no means handsome but he exuded power and ruthlessness and I could see at first glance that he was not the sort of man it was wise to cross. So, accordingly, I said nothing when he took my hand, leaned over it and I felt his mouth, hot and wet, upon my wrist.

The seat beside him was empty and I smiled gratitude as he bid me to fill it. As he filled my cup, the fluid like liquid rubies I pretended I was flattered and lifted it, holding his gaze for a moment before drinking. At the other end of the table Cynfeddw was still prancing about on the board. His father leaned back in his chair revelling in his son's antics as if he were part of the entertainment. I shot him a loaded look and with a jerk of my head ordered our son to resume his seat. Then I turned to Penda, assuming my best smile, wondering how on earth I was supposed to engage such an alarming man in polite conversation.

He was picking scraps of meat from his teeth with his dagger. Then he rinsed his mouth with mead and spat it into the rushes, slamming down his cup and belching loudly. I offered him a golden pear, dripping with honey but he declined it with a shake of his head. 'A fine hall you have, Madam, not as fine as my own but it comes a close second. You will have to let me entertain you at my hall one of these days.'

His eyes were fastened on my breasts and I knew he wasn't including my husband in his imagined hospitality. I drank from my cup again and looked across the hall to where a trio of tumblers had appeared from nowhere to cartwheel across the floor. The hall erupted into laughter and Cynfeddw climbed back on the table the better to see. From the corner of my eye I saw Cadafael drag him back by the breeches and cast a wary look in my direction.

My jaws began to ache with the strain of smiling but I could see further down the table that Ffreur showed no such effort. Smiling came naturally to her and she laughed uproariously at everything and clapped in delight at the antics of the tumblers. I turned to pay them closer attention just as one tossed the other high in the air so that his spinning body barely missed the swinging overhead lanterns.

Opening my eyes wide, I turned to Penda, whose mouth was open in appreciation, displaying a half-chewed mouthful of pork. He clapped a hand on my knee and roared with laughter again. 'Oh,' he cried, wiping his eyes, 'I don't remember when I have seen anything to equal that.' He kept his hand on my knee, exploring my thigh and I let him continue, knowing that it was imperative we did not offend him. We needed his strength in this coming war and I would have to bear his attention for as long as I could.

To my left, my brother Cynwraith noticed nothing amiss but drank steadily, a quiet man in rowdy company. When Penda topped up my cup again, I pretended to drink from it, smiling at him over the rim as I sipped delicately. He put down his own cup and wiped his mouth on his sleeve, his eye fixed on my bosom.

'Cadafael is a lucky man, Madam. I never knew he possessed such riches.' His eyes shifted to the thick torc that glistened on my collarbone. 'He keeps secrets from me, Madam. Friends should share their treasures don't you think?'

In any other man it would have been a compliment but there was something predatory in his eye. I suppressed a shiver and he laughed again, enjoying my discomfort and reinforcing the pressure on my thigh. I feared I'd be bruised come morning but I laughed with him and dipped my face desperately to my cup again as he outdid himself in impressing me.

'I've slaughtered many men, Madam; Kings, thegns, beggars … and priests, lots of priests.' I tried to appear suitably captivated but while he leered at me, I looked about for an excuse to escape.

To my great relief I saw Ffreur frantically signalling for my company. She jerked her head toward the privy, silently asking me to join her there so, very much relieved, I stood up and Penda's hand fell away.

'Excuse me, Lord, I have need to retire for a short while. Pray, keep company with my brother until I return.' He turned grudgingly away, grumbling in his greasy beard.

I caught up with Ffreur in the anti-chamber where arrangements were laid out for the comfort of the women. My sister turned large, reproachful eyes on me.

'Gracious, Heledd, why on earth are you flirting with Penda?' I scrubbed at a greasy stain on my skirts and glared at her through my fringe.

'He is flirting with me, Ffreur. Just look at my new tunic, ruined. Soon Angharad will go about better dressed than I.'

She bent down to examine the damage.

'It is not so bad. I expect Gwarw will have the skill to clean it. Anyway, you have other clothes.' She stood up, stretching her back, as stiff with sitting as I. The pose accentuated her hand-span waist and tiny breasts. She still had the body of a child and made me feel cumbersome. I took out a comb and began to tidy her hair, in no hurry to return to the hall. If Penda felt the need to maul Cadafael's women why couldn't he choose the whore and leave the wife alone?

Removing one of my slippers which were a little tight, I rubbed at the sore place on my heel then, hitching up my skirts, I pissed in the nearest pot while Ffreur stood waiting.

'I suppose we must return,' she said, 'the musicians are on next.' Wiping myself on my petticoat, I arranged my skirts and tweaked at my hair.

'Yes, I suppose so, I am coming,' I said and followed her from the room into the hall but, as I hurried to catch up with her, Penda stepped from nowhere, filling the adjoining passage with his bulk. Ffreur, the sorry little coward, fled, leaving me to his mercy.

'I thought I'd lost you, Madam.' He stepped closer and it was all I could do not to take a step backward.

'Oh, I wasn't long,' I said playfully. A huge beard, knotted with beads and bones, screened his lips and when he yawned suddenly, the inside of his mouth showed extraordinarily red against its darkness.

'I think it must be bedtime, Madam.' His eyes bored into mine and he stood so close that I could see the wiry hairs springing from his nose. The stench of his lust was appalling.

'No, not nearly, the night is young, it is hardly past dusk.' I gestured to the window and as I did so, he stepped forward and snaked an arm about me, pressing my body against his. I leaned away from him and let out a squeal.

'With a woman like you, Madam, I think it is always bed time.' Laughter gusted down his nose and, fastened against his body as I was, I could not move. Knowing that resistance would only fire his lust I tried not to struggle when he clamped his mouth over mine. I tasted the greasiness of his beard while his hands, as large as flails, simultaneously fastened upon my buttocks. I was forced to bear it, could scarcely draw breath and the noxious kiss continued for so long I thought I should faint. When, at last he released me, I almost collapsed and he let out a bellow of laughter, thinking my weakness a response to his overwhelming masculine charm.

'We will finish this business later, Madam.' He slapped my arse and strode back into the hall, belching loudly as he went. Needing a few moments to regain my composure, I let out a long breath and smoothed my gown and as I did so I caught a movement from the corner of my eye.

'Angharad. Oh, did you see that? The gall of the man, Ughh!' She stood with her back to the wall, a jug of wine clasped to her chest, her black eyes watching me accusingly. She did not make reply and without sparing her another thought, I left her and hurried back to the hall.

The air was full of smoke and it was difficult to make out the musicians assembling before the dais, ready to sing. The hubbub of voices rose and fell in waves as the servants began to carry in the next course and the revellers fell upon the food. The scraps were thrown into the rushes and the dogs set up a squabble over the choicest leavings.

I looked about for Ffreur who had stopped to speak to some of the elders. I could hear the old woman enthusing about the likeness Ffreur bore to our mother and, unwilling to be trapped in tedious conversation, I quickly passed them by. Lifting my skirts, I prepared to ascend the steps of the dais and Penda heaved himself upright in his chair at my approach making my heart sink as I faced the task of fending him off for another four hours.

I looked about me for a diversion and noticed Cynfeddw wrestling with his nurse who was trying to take him to bed and, instead of taking my seat, I bypassed the visiting King to join Cadafael and my son. With hands on hips, I cast a disapproving eye upon him until he stopped struggling.

'Good night, Cynfeddw,' I said firmly and he scowled before placing a sulky kiss upon my proffered cheek.

Good night, Mother.'

Ffreur was still engaged in conversation but, seeing them as a lesser evil to Penda, I changed my mind and went to join them. Ffreur looked up and saw me, indicating to the old woman that I approached but as I drew near, the sound of a harp rippled, like a flooding tide, across the hall.

I stopped. Ffreur paused mid-sentence, her hand flying to her mouth and my own heart almost ceased its rhythm. I fought to breathe as, with pain in my throat, I looked across the hall to where, burnished gold by the light of the flaming fire, Osian stood waiting to sing.

Three

I could not move. He did not look for me although he must have known I was there but when his voice erupted into the smoky air, I knew his words were for me alone. Tears stung my eyes and a confusion of throbbing tenderness simmered in the pit of my stomach as he sang about a maid enamoured of a travelling player. But their love was forbidden by her father and they were forced to part. As Osian sang, each syllable, every note that floated across the void between us, vibrated with truth.

Now, I recognised my dream beneath the lynden tree as a foretelling of the future. Osian and I would be together again, and soon. How and when did not matter for he was there, in the circle of my vision and my ears and heart were full of his music.

He sang several more times during the course of the night and, although I resumed my place at Penda's side, I paid him scant notice. I no longer minded when he recommenced his intimate exploration of my thigh my mind was far away, roaming the night skies with Osian. Poor Penda, although he continued to monopolise me for the rest of the evening, I have no memory of his words. I leaned forward in my seat, my elbows on the board and rested my chin in my hands while my eyes drank in the beauty of the minstrel.

That night I tossed and turned, rose from the bed to pace the chamber until at last, I gave up the struggle and threw on a cloak and slid from the room. In the hall men, over-full with mead snored, some with their heads on the table and some sprawled about the floor. Dogs crept among them, feasting upon scraps dropped in the rushes and in the far corner one of Penda's men coupled ferociously with a hearth wench. They did not notice my presence and as I slipped out into the night they reached the pinnacle of their pleasure, their cries of delight masking the sound of my footsteps.

It was a cold, bright night, the idiot face of the moon floating in a sea of stars. Keeping a wary eye out for observers I hurried across the enclosure, stopping suddenly when I detected a sound. With my heart beating hard I scanned the precinct hard by the stables.

A figure was pacing back and forth, muttering curses beneath his breath. At once I recognised the straggling hair, the brawny chest, the glint of golden arm-rings. I slid down the wall into the shadows and bit my lip, a dim recollection of agreeing to Penda's proposal of a lover's tryst. With my mind so full of Osian, had I agreed?

Indecisively, I waited, trapped in a pit of my own making, wondering what on earth I could do. If he caught sight of me he would think I had come to fulfil my promise. The memory of that single kiss flashed upon my inner eye and my stomach revolted at the thought. I choked back vomit. He was more repellent than Cadafael.

I hesitated for some time, watching his impatience increase until his curses grew louder until, with an exclamation of frustration, he turned his back, loosened his leggings and stood ready to piss against the stable. I took my chance and, at the first sound of his water splashing against the wall, I dived into the night and sped toward the outer gate.

The moon, suddenly shy, hid briefly behind scudding clouds and the buildings that clustered to the settlement wall became indistinct in the darkness. I hunched in my cloak and assumed a limp, keeping to the perimeter and once safely through, I slipped onto the hillside and stood for a while regaining my breath. The night was bright and cold, my exertion visible like dragon's breath.

Then the clouds lifted, briefly illuminating the landscape. Far below, the waters of the mere glimmered silver and the wood clustered in dense shadow at the foot of the hill. I would go to Ceri. She would work some magic and tell me what I should do.

Dodging across open ground, I hurried to the safety of the wood, my cloak pulled high about my face. I slid into the shelter of the trees, slowing as the darkness grew deeper and creeping blindly onward, my arms held out before me, unable to see my way ahead. When someone roughly seized my left hand I screamed aloud, struggling to loosen his grip.

A fist held me fast, dragging me forward, my heart thumping in fear as I realised Penda had followed. His pace was brisk and I stumbled behind him, the aroma of loamy soil rising from the disturbed woodland floor. When we reached a place where the canopy opened above our heads and the light of moon filtered through the branches, he stopped and spun me around.

'Heledd.' His lips were on my neck, his arms tight about me. I could not speak. 'I have thought of you every day, every hour.'

I threw back my head, offering my throat.

'Every minute,' I groaned before our lips locked together. At last, desperate to breathe, I pulled away and looked into Osian's face. 'Are you mazed? You risk your life coming here like this.'

His eyes glistened with joy, his recklessness contagious.

'I don't think I care. Oh, my love, when Cynddylan asked me to accompany him here, I could not refuse. My life is miserable without you. Death would be a small price to pay.'

He began to push my kirtle from my shoulders and it took all my will to stop him. Lifting his face from my bosom he looked at me questioningly, his lips parted as he panted desperately.

'Not here, Osian. Not like this, as if I were a whore. It is unsafe and unsuitable,' I pleaded. 'Let me make arrangements. If this is to be our last time together, I want it to be perfect. I will send one to you tomorrow that I trust.'

He groaned and pushed a hand through his hair before nodding.

'Make it soon, Heledd, soon.'

He was upon me again, his fingers knotted in my hair, his tongue wet upon my skin. My body screamed with longing. I wanted to give in to him and let him take me, there on the woodland floor and it took all my will to wrench myself away. I backed off.

'Tomorrow,' I whispered and, turning from him, whirled along the path. He called after me but I did not allow myself to look back. I burst through Ceri's door, with my soul on fire, breathless and dishevelled.

Her raven shrieked and something stirred in her sleeping place. With a curse she crawled from her bed and peered at me through the darkness, noting my heaving chest and dishevelled hair.

'My queen,' she cackled without surprise, poking the fire back to life. 'What brings you here so hot …and at this hour?'

She gestured for me to sit and I tipped a cat from the stool and perched, hugging my knees and leaning toward her.

'You must help me, Ceri. I have need of a very great favour. I will reward you well. Better than ever before.'

She handed me a cup of something warm and comforting and settled opposite me at the fire.

'You had better tell me all about it,' she said and, fixing me with a keen eye, she prepared to listen to my tale.

Ceri's hut was not the most obvious trysting place but I could think of nowhere safer. The settlement was accustomed to women sneaking through the wood at nightfall for a potion or a charm against evil and there was no reason for Osian's movements to be monitored. If we were careful all should be well.

I dismissed my women early, pleading the headache and threatened Gwarw with death should she admit anyone to my chamber, even the King. She scolded me as against her will she scented my body, brushed out my hair so that it crackled and shone. When I encased myself in her drab grey cloak, she scowled and called me a slattern. She believed my assignation was with Penda and, to my shame, I did not put her right.

'Shut up, Gwarw,' I said, leaving a kiss on her forehead. 'I am a grown woman and keep my own counsel. I will be back before dawn.'

I crept along the path and through the door of the hut. The interior was dark, the aroma that resembled decaying mushrooms familiar to me now. Ceri had made herself scarce and Osian was already waiting, poking the sulky fire with a stick. He sprang from his stool and dragged me into his arms. This time I could not have stopped him had I wanted to.

There was no waiting.

Feverishly we struggled with lacings and fastenings and when we were full naked, fell laughing into Ceri's malodorous bed. He was ready, we both were, and he took me in haste and with little finesse but we had no time to spare for the gentle rituals of love. It was not long before we lay gasping side by side upon the straw-stuffed pillow, my hair snarled and my heart racing like a leverets'.

He shifted onto his hip, resting his head on his hand and stroking my belly with the other.

'I cannot believe we are really here, you must tell me everything that has happened.' He spoke quietly, unwilling to break the spell that lay upon us.

Glad of the poor light, I told him of my heartbreak at leaving Pengwern, my distaste for Cadafael and the meagre satisfactions I had as Gwynedd's queen.

'I think of you, Osian, in the midst of night when I am alone. I stare at the moon and wonder if you are seeing it too.'

The firelight glinted on his hair as he smiled his warm, slow smile.

'I usually am.' His voice was husky. 'Sometimes I curse myself for not risking the wrath of your brothers and speaking out, laying my claim to you.'

An alternative life flashed before my eyes, a life in which I married him, lived the life of a commoner. It was a heart-warming picture but I blinked it away and sat up, scooping my hair back into a knot. My breasts stood out proud and when his gaze fastened upon them his smile negated the moistness of his eye.

'I know my duty, Osian. I was raised to be a queen and I try to be dutiful. I want to make my brothers proud. Oh, but when I am with you all that disappears. It is only when we are together that I can ever truly be Heledd.'

'Don't,' he knelt up, wiped a tear from my cheek. 'Don't cry. There will be time for weeping later.'

His kiss was gentle. I turned up my face to him, leaned toward him, mutely asking for more. His lips moved across my face and along the curve of my neck. Lifting my hair, he left a trail of saliva between my shoulder blades and along my spine, making me shiver. Then, he shifted round, sinking his face into my belly, gripping my hips, his tongue tracing the tell-tale tracks around my navel. I winced a little, hoping he should not see the marks that proved I had borne another man's child but the feeling was fleeting.

My skin quivered, goose pimples following in the wake of his mouth, my breath catching in my throat, my breasts rising and falling as I waited for his lips … and for his tongue. Arching toward him, I tangled my fingers in his damp hair, letting out a squeak of delight as he ensnared me in tortuous delight. I opened my mouth, tilted back my head, my body a dancing cataract, cascading with delight. Then I slumped back, sated, a foolish smile on my face and he slithered up my body, wiping his mouth on the back of his hand.

'Osian,' I flushed. 'My goodness.'

I did not have the words I needed and he let out a burst of laughter, pulling me into his arms again.

'Where did you learn to do that?' I asked, but I was glad when he declined to answer.

I had spent many wakeful nights during our years apart, missing him, pacing the floor, recalling his face, remembering his touch. Those nights had seemed endless, my misery frozen in unforgiving darkness but that first joyous night we shared at Ceri's hut passed in the blinking of an eye and, before we knew it, the cockerels were screeching in the dawn.

He watched me dress, mourning each layer of clothing that I put on and then he rose to help me fasten my cloak. It seemed awkward to stand fully clothed against his nakedness, as if I were his shameless seducer. He gently kissed my cheek, his hand lingering, stroking a reluctant path down my face until it fell limp at his side.

I opened the door and stepped outside. As I crept along the fern fringed path, the dew soaking my thin slippers my heart hung like a stone. The night had passed so quickly and we might never be together again. Suddenly I remembered a thousand things I had left unsaid and in all my life I had never felt worse than at that moment of parting.

At the curve in the path, where the trees began to thin, I turned back for a last look. He raised a hand, his body gleaming alabaster in the half-light and his hair shining like spun gold but, as I stepped into the sunshine the darkness closed in upon him, extinguishing the joy from my world.

Four

I need not have worried for we did enjoy other meetings, fleeting times that always ended too soon. The war council lasted many weeks as Cadafael and my brothers wrangled with Penda about the best course of action and I managed to spend three nights in seven with him in Ceri's noxious bed. It was not long before my impatience for the day to end so that I could slip away to be with him piqued Ffreur's curiosity.

'What is it, Heledd? You are as jumpy as a louse.'

'No, I'm not,' I retorted, my face burning. She made a disbelieving sound but I bent my head to my stitching again and changed the subject, calling Angharad to bring refreshments.

She placed a tray of nuts and berries on the table before retreating to her seat and taking up her distaff again. It was quiet in the chamber, the only sound the crackle of flames and the gentle tic of Gwarw's snores. I let my mind slip back to the previous night when, impatient to be with him, I had arrived at Ceri's far too early. Tonight, although it would be so hard, I must force myself to wait until it was fully dark. It was to be our last night, perhaps forever, for in the morning the men would ride away to make war on the North Umbrian King.

Ceri had a new fur-lined cloak and some sturdy boots and her winter stores were replete with grain and turnips. With my life balanced precariously in her withered palm I had paid her well to ensure her loyalty. So familiar had I become with the path to her cottage that I could find my way along it blindfold. She greeted me with a crooked smile, handed me a fortifying drink and watched as I drank it. She looked up suddenly, alert to Osian's approach before I was although he was still some way off.

'Oh, he is a fine looking fellow,' she leered at him as he turned the bend in the path. 'Were I a young gel I might have to fight you for him.'

A laugh consumed her and, as she rocked to and fro on her stool.

I smiled too. 'You forget, Ceri, I was raised in a family of boys and can wrestle with the best of them.'

We chuckled a while longer and then she sobered, munched on her gums for a moment. Then she nodded at my stomach. 'What'll you do about the babe you carry?'

My hands flew instinctively to my belly. 'What do you mean?'

I stared at her, fear and joy mingling in my bosom. Surely it was far too soon for any pregnancy. She reached out and balanced my breasts in her palms.

'I mean, child, that you are carrying the musician's babe. Shall I make up a potion to be rid of it?'

My stool flew away as I sprang to my feet. 'No, my God, Ceri! Oh, what shall I do?'

The thought of aborting Osian's child was hateful; there must be another way. I glanced from the door to where my lover turning in at the gate as Ceri patted my arm.

'Don't worry about it now. You just enjoy your last night together. We will find a way out of it, you and I.' Then, snatching her cloak from its hook by the door and winking appreciatively at Osian as their paths crossed on the threshold, she left us alone.

'What is it? Why are you crying?' He came to me, lifted my hair and left a kiss where my neck and shoulders joined.

I dashed away a tear. 'I wasn't aware that I was. It is just that this is our last meeting. This time our parting may be forever.'

It was easy to lie to him. He stood behind me at the hearth and put his hands round me, cupping my breasts. 'Nay,' he whispered. 'Not forever, I swear it.'

That night our lovemaking was prolonged and intense, as if he sought to possess as much of me as he could in the time remaining to us. When we parted at dawn I crawled, miserable and exhausted, back to my chamber and told Gwarw to plead sickness so I should be spared the ordeal of watching him ride away. I didn't give a thought to the fact that my husband and brothers were riding away also, perhaps never to return and with grief too deep for tears, I lay curled into myself like a dormouse beneath the covers while Gwarw, still believing that I mourned for Penda, patted my hand and shuffled off to make my excuses.

The door opened, letting in a gust of wind and I opened my eyes to find Ffreur at my bedside. She gripped my hand. 'Please, Heledd, get up. This is not like you. You are scaring me.'

Through my tangled hair I saw her anxious face and felt a jolt of guilt. I had lain abed for nigh on a week, refusing proper food and only taking a little water. I may as well be dead as live an empty life. Ffreur held out a jewelled cup. 'Come, Heledd, sit up and drink this. The sun is shining, look. Come along, do it for love of me.'

Reluctantly I pulled myself onto my pillows, squinting at the daylight pouring through the horn-glazed window and took the cup, letting the fortifying wine flow through my body.

She looked pleased, patted my hand. 'There, that is better.' Her eyes smiled and I did not pull my hand away.

'Heledd,' she said, her voice hesitant, her eyes troubled. 'Gwarw says that you are enamoured of Penda.' Her look darted about the chamber and, satisfied that we were alone, she dropped her voice to a whisper. 'But it isn't Penda, is it? It's that other fellow; the minstrel?'

My pulse sounded loudly in my ear, my breath shortened but I was too weary to lie to her. 'How did you know?'

I drew my hand away and looked down at my sore nails that I had gnawed in my misery but she snatched it back again, held it firm against her breast.

'The first time that he came to Cynddylan's Hall you were changed afterward. I suspected something then but you would not confide in me. And then we were married and I thought you would forget him but when he came here last month, well, I watched your face and I recognised the way you were feeling. I feel that way for Iestyn. You are in love, Heledd, and I know you too well to think it could be with a man like Penda.'

My resolve broke, my chin quivered like a child's. 'Oh, Ffreur, I don't know how I can live without him? My whole life is bland, like an unseasoned feast. If I did not know such feelings existed it would be easier but I cannot live everyday …'

My words dissolved and Ffreur took me in her arms, rocking me back and forth as if I were her child.

Five

It took a few good meals and plenty of mead until I was clear sighted enough to see what course had to be taken. By the month's end I was vomiting profusely in the mornings and my courses had not come. Ceri was right. I was with child. When there was no one by to witness, I summoned Angharad.

She slipped through the door and when she saw me, her mouth widened and she joined me at the fireside. She looked well. Her body had filled out with better food and warmth.

'Lady,' she said, sketching a brief curtsey. 'How are you feeling, I heard you have been sick.'

'I am well enough.' That day there was something about her manner that irritated me but I put it down to my condition. She sat at my feet on Gwarw's stool, her head high and her expression open and all of a sudden I realised that she was comfortable, even happy in her role. I saw that what had begun as an abhorrence to her was now, rather pleasing.

I decided to be blunt. 'Angharad, I want you to plead sickness for a few weeks. Should my husband require your services you are to be indisposed.'

I did not miss the flash of resentment before she replied, 'Sickness, Lady, whatever for?'

Her eyes gleamed, darkly inquisitive but I did not deign to answer. Her duty was to do my bidding. I shrugged off her question.

'Just be too ill to attend him should he need you. I will inform you should I change my mind.'

She recognised her dismissal and stood up and bobbed her knees, her expression sulky, her eyes guarded.

'Yes, Lady,' she murmured and, making a perfunctory bow, left my presence and I spared her no more thought but turned my mind to the distasteful task ahead with Cadafael.

I managed to get him alone one evening as he returned from the privy.

'Oh,' I said, feigning pleasant surprise. 'My Lord, good evening.' I let him enjoy the full force of my smile. 'We see so little of each other these days; it is a great pity that war takes you from us so often. You must be glad to be home.'

His response was guarded. 'Indeed, Madam, I had not realised my company held such value.'

'You are my husband, the father of my child, of course I value you.'

He looked down his nose, assessing my intent. 'And I you, Lady.' Uncertainly, keeping his eye upon me, he bowed and after a pause asked, 'and how is our son?'

This was surer ground and simpler to select words that would please.

'Oh, he is well, Lord. He grows apace and his skill with his wooden sword overshadows that of all the other boys. I pride myself that he is like his father and I hope that in the future his brothers will prove to be as strong.'

I stretched out a hand to assess the strength of his bicep, cocking an eyebrow in admiration. He coughed, disconcertedly shuffling his feet and as I walked away I cast a crooked, lusty grin over my shoulder.

I knew he would come and that evening, shooing all the women from my chamber, I waited for the roistering hall to sober. I wondered if he would be drunk and wished with all heart that I was, but when it came his footstep was regular and steady. I tossed off my grief and pinned on a shiny welcome.

He hesitated just inside the door, cast his gaze about the room and hid his surprise at finding me alone. I swung my legs from the bed and moved toward him, offered him a cup of welcome and the fool, still unsuspicious of our former dealings, drank deeply.

'Madam,' he said and, unwilling to lengthen an unpleasant interlude, I moved into his arms, reaching for his kiss.

At first his lips remained stiff, resisting but I pressed myself against him, wound my arms about his neck. It did not take long for his ardour to rise and once he realised his manhood wasn't going to fail him, his breath grew hoarse as he fumbled with his leggings. Part of me wanted to fight him off, to flee the chamber and cast myself upon my brother's mercy but, instead, clinging to the knowledge that I must protect Osian's son, I cleaved to my husband, feigning ecstasy.

He rumpled my gown up above my hips and, hoisting me onto the mattress, entered me quickly and without affection. His enjoyment was rough and vocal and he didn't seem to notice the tears oozing from the corners of my eyes. I buried my face in his shoulder and bit my lip and as he reached his peak, I turned my head away. When I was with my lover I never felt like an adulterer but in sleeping with my husband the guilt became so strong I could not banish Osian's anguished face from my mind.

He stayed until morning, a thing he had never done before. All night I sat wakeful on my pillows with my knees folded in my arms and watched him snore. His hair fell dark against the pillow; his head was thrown back, his throat bared, as vulnerable as a child.

I spoke harshly to myself, silently reasoning that he was not a bad husband, had never done a thing to hurt me. It was not his fault he was unskilled in the art of love. I scolded myself that I must try harder. I was the one with evil intent, the one that plotted against him, unmanned him and used him intimately to screen my own transgressions. He could not help that he was not the man I loved.

I slid down the bed in the darkness and, cupping my hands over my belly, I sent a pulse of love to the child, curled, wormlike in my womb. The babe would be raised as my husband's son, a brother to Cynfeddw and, blind to the depths of my own treachery, I felt little shame for it.

In the morning, Cadafael woke cheerfully and rolled me onto my back to assuage his morning needs while I lay passive beneath him, waiting for an end, wondering what tunic I should wear.

I surmised that three visits to my bed should do it and then I could feign sickness and send him back to Angharad. But, three weeks and many visits later, he did not stop coming. In the end I let him see me hang off the side of the bed and spew my morning herring into the rushes. His lip curled in disgust.

'What ails you, woman?' He banged on Gwarw's closet door and as she crawled from sleep to attend me I sent him a weak smile.

'I think I must have quickened with your child, Husband,' I said, wiping the vomit from my lips. For a moment he looked surprised but then straightened up.

'That was quick work,' he said and, slapping Gwarw on the back, he strutted whistling, from the chamber.

I slumped on my pillow and gestured for a drink. I had done it, he was fooled and no suspicion could fall upon me now. My mission accomplished, I sent a prayer of thanks to whichever god was listening.

Ffreur came to my apartment, fresh and cleansed from confession.

'Still abed, Heledd? At this time?' She did not miss the triumph in my eyes and raised her brows questioningly until I told her my news, expecting her envy.

'I am feeling sickly, Ffreur, I think I am with child again.'

She threw herself at me, making no attempt to hide her easy tears.

'Oh, I am so glad for you, Heledd.' She hesitated, glanced quickly about the room. 'When do you expect the confinement?'

'Mid-summer, I think.' I rubbed a hand across my belly and grinned smugly.

'Heledd,' she leaned forward, her braids like golden ropes. 'It is the musician's child you carry isn't it?'

It was not a question and I saw no point in lying. I nodded, filled with a sudden fierce joy.

'It is Ffreur and only you, I and one other know of it.'

Six

At this point, more than any other, the drums of war beat loudly and this time it was civil war. Oswiu and Penda must wait, for the followers of Gwynedd's old King had banded together against Cadafael and our kingdom was in danger. I was just a child when Cadwallon ap Cadfan was killed, leaving an infant son to govern the Kingdom. Cadafael, little more than a youth with a young man's lust for power, had ousted him and taken the throne for himself but, now grown to manhood, Cadwaladr returned to win back his Kingdom.

The settlement rang with the tramp of feet, messengers arriving and leaving at the dead of night. The clash of sword practice, the unfurling of banners, horns sounding. Cadafael spent less time in my bed and more in the company of his hearth troop and pretended to be confident about the coming battle. But I knew there were those among us ready to betray him and creep to the camp of the enemy.

My brothers sent assurances, pledging to beat back the encroaching armies and uphold Cadafael's claim to Gwynedd and the inheritance of our son, Cynfeddw. While the turmoil of politics rattled on above my head, my mind was filled with excitement of the forthcoming birth. I kept to the women's quarters, stroking the rise of my belly, dreaming dreams of my child's red haired father.

Childbearing is a time of great risk and I have lost many a friend and cousin to childbed fever, and more often, the new-born babe itself perished. I had seen many a swaddled bundle tucked quietly beneath the hearth but I bore no fears, either for myself or for Osian's child. I knew that, with Ceri's help, I would bear the ordeal well and my child would thrive.

By early summer my belly jutted like the ship's prow and, smug in my happiness, I could barely wait for the confinement. Ffreur and I counted down the weeks while Gwarw prepared everything I would require for the lying in. I had ensured well in advance that Ceri would attend me and, thus prepared, was able to look forward to greeting my son unhampered by worry.

This time when the pains came I recognised them for what they were and sent Gwarw to summon Ffreur and Ceri. With everything in readiness, I ordered the fire to be stoked and settled at the hearth to wait.

It was dusk. From the open door of my bower I could see the June sun melting into the distant sea. Ffreur crept into the room. 'Where have you been?' I asked tetchily as she took her place beside me and began to massage oil into my belly.

'I settled the children into their beds. Gosh, Heledd, your stomach is as taut as a drum.'

I shifted a little, fidgeting my legs while her tiny hands followed the line of the blue circles that Ceri had drawn on the contours of the bulge.

'I will be glad when it's over, how much longer?' I asked.

In the corner Ceri was rummaging in her basket. She drew out a ball of twine, a bowl and a knife and put them on a low table near the bed.

'Let's have a look see, shall we?' She parted my knees, inserted a bony finger and pressed down. 'The doors be opening, he won't be long now. When you feel like pushing we'll move onto the furs.'

Ffreur grinned. 'There, you see, not long now.'

I closed my eyes and lay against the pillows, the next pain already nudging at the base of my spine. I blew out a sharp breath, scowling a little.

Ffreur raised an eyebrow. 'Is another one coming? Here we go then.' She increased the pressure of her hands, her ministrations both soothing and annoying at the same time. I sat up a little, spread my legs, puffed out my cheeks and then gave a groan. The pains were growing stronger.

In the four years since Cynfeddw's birth I had forgotten the agony of it all, and when the tightening in my back and the nausea began in earnest, just like the last time I wept like a child for my mother.

'Ceri,' I sobbed. 'Do something. I cannot take much more.'

'Yes, you can, girl,' she replied, throwing another handful of herbs onto the fire. The rich aroma immediately filled the air, soothing my mind a little and helping my muscles to relax between assaults. It eased me for a while but soon, when I was on the brink of screaming again, she brought me a cup of something fragrant. I sipped at it, the hot liquid filling my mouth with the taste of the woodland floor before burning a trail to my belly.

I slept then, only stirring to fight against each new pain. Ffreur did not leave my side. She bathed the sweat from my brow, kneaded the seat of my agony and murmured sympathy when the anguish gripped me.

After what seemed a lifetime each spasm was followed by an urge to push. It is not a feeling to be denied. Ceri noted the gritted teeth and straining muscles.

'Come child,' she ordered. 'Down upon the blanket.'

I moved stiffly, not properly in control of my limbs. The fur was soft on my knees, the flames in the brazier leaping on the chamber walls. Gwarw lowered her creaking joints to the floor beside Ceri and I while Ffreur summoned Hild from her chores. We formed a ring, our combined strength reducing my burden, my pain pouring into them and their strength passing into me.

Ceri began to chant. I recalled the refrain from my first confinement but could not join in for my agony was too great. The conjoined voices of the women, the aroma of the herbs and the sensation of many oily hands on my body sent me into a kind of trance. I was aware of all that happened yet, at the same time, I was detached from it, freed from the burden of labour.

I looked down, as if from high above and could clearly see us, a ring of females engaged in female business. I saw myself, great with child, encircled by those I loved. I felt no pain as I floated near the rafters and watched myself throw back my head, open my legs and let out a primitive, animal cry as my child slithered onto the blanket.

Quite suddenly I was back in my body, aware of frantic hands severing the cord and placing the screaming, pulsing child upon my breast. The trauma was done. I smelled my son's sweet wet hair, placed my hand upon his wrinkled body and wept with joy.

While Gwarw and Hild washed the blood from my limbs and clothed me in a fresh kirtle I refused to relinquish the child. The women set the room to rights while Ceri bent her head over a bowl that held the afterbirth. She poked it with her finger.

'A fine specimen,' she remarked. 'Can I keep it?'

I nodded. I had no care for that for I was absorbed in my son. She tucked it away, knotted her shawl about her and opened the door. 'I will return in the morning, just to ensure all is well with you.'

I waved an absent hand. Ffreur peeled back the edge of the blanket, the better to see him.

'Oh, Heledd, he is lovely.' Looking down at the crumpled face, the halo of wet, red hair, the miniscule fingers that gripped my own, I had to agree.

He was Osian's son and he was mine.

An hour later Cadafael put his head around the door.

'Where is my son? Can I see him?' He stepped over the threshold and came toward the bed, seeming huge and very masculine in the feminine space. He loomed over to where the child was tucked in the crook of my arm, feasting upon my breast, his mouth unable to accommodate such a large brown nipple.

My husband peered through the dim light, put out a finger to stroke his cheek. 'So tiny,' he said. 'A fine addition to our family. Well done, Heledd. Everything went as it should? You are well?'

I nodded, putting a finger to my lips to indicate I did not wish to disturb my son. Cadafael pulled up a stool, perched at the side of the bed.

'My mother had red hair,' he said. It was the first time I ever heard him speak of his mother whom, gossip said, was a commoner. I looked at him in surprise and he smiled, his lips stretched wide and I wished so much that he were Osian.

While my husband admired my son Gwarw crept about the room tidying things away and Cadafael signalled to her to bring him a drink. He raised his cup.

'To future children,' he grinned. 'A daughter next time, perhaps.' Then he slurped his wine, stood up and kissed first my forehead and then my son's. Jealousy twisted my gut and I cradled the child tight to me, moving him as far from Cadafael as I could.

'Don't,' I glared at him. 'You will wake him and I will be up all night soothing him.' He held up his hands in submission.

'Sorry, wife, I didn't think. I will leave you to sleep, both of you and see you anon.'

Seven

But it was many weeks before I saw him again. The very next day word came that Cadwaladr's armies had attacked Llanfaes, the royal llys on Yns Môn. There was great upheaval in the palace, the shouts and trumpeting of the army echoing into the chamber as the army prepared to ride in haste to repulse the invaders.

In the men's absence life progressed as usual and I spared them little thought. Confident in Cadafael's ability to vanquish his foe, I knew he would return and had no fears that I would be widowed. And as it turned out, I was right not to worry although by the time they did come back, I had already been churched and resumed my duties as Queen.

It was September and the preparations for winter were underway when we first spotted the cavalcade of horses bearing my husband home. My heart sank but I smoothed my apron and prepared dutifully to greet him.

He slid from his horse and looked about, nodding appreciatively at the bushels of grain, the drying meat and the barrels of apples and pears. I wove my way between the waiting carts, dodging slaves bent beneath the weight of heavy sacks. He looked thinner and his beard was more unkempt than usual but, other than that, he was just the same.

'Madam,' he greeted me. 'How are my sons?'

I smiled blithely and held out an arm to bid him follow me to the hall.

'They are well, My Lord. If Cynfeddw worked as hard at his lessons as he does at evading his tutor he would do better.'

Cadafael's laughter was infectious but I controlled my smile. 'And the babe? Is he named yet? Does he thrive?' My heart lilted a little as it always did when I thought of him.

'I named him Hedyn, My Lord, after my long-dead brother. I hope you approve? Shall I summon the nurse to bring them to you?'

He threw his gauntlets onto the table and sat down.

'No, not now. I need food and a bath. I will see them later. The campaign was a success, Cadwaladr is exiled and the threat is now passed.' He put his feet on a stool and crossed his ankles. 'That leaves us free to continue the war against Oswiu. We might as well strike while our blood is up. Where is Iestyn? He was with me when I rode in.'

I cast my eyes to Heaven. 'Where do you think he is? He is with Ffreur, making up for lost time.'

Our eyes met and I flushed slightly at his meaningful grin.

'We should be doing likewise, Wife, but I can wait if you can.' He lifted his shirt and scratched his belly, capturing a louse and squeezing it between his finger nails. 'I could do with a bath.'

We both looked up at a sound by the door and Angharad emerged from behind the curtain. She had changed her gown, combed her hair and I was suddenly aware of my soiled apron and dusty hem. Cadafael stood up, hesitated, looking from me to Angharad and back again. He coughed to fill the awkward silence, then turned toward me sharply, bowing over my hand and I thought I saw an apology in his eye as he left a kiss upon it.

'I will go and freshen up and come to your chamber in a while, Madam.'

Angharad barely reached his shoulder. She turned and walked away with him, her upright body diminutive next to his and I saw triumph in the set of her shoulders, the angle of her head. Left alone in the hall I felt a pang of jealousy.

Eight

Winter rolled in, swathing the settlement in mist, battering it with rain. We huddled within doors, wrapped in furs and tried to keep the children amused with stories and songs. The dogs, disgruntled by the howling winds that lifted the thatch and set the roof timbers creaking, were restless and disputes between them were frequent.

We were sitting round the hearth listening to Cadafael tell the tale of his first hunting kill. The children sat among the dogs on the furs, like a litter of puppies, each vying with the other for the warmest spot. They tilted their faces to their father, entranced with his words.

It was a story we had heard many times but the thrill of it did not diminish with the retelling and, if any noticed that he embellished it with each fresh airing, none of us minded or remarked upon it. He was living the tale he told and his audience was enthralled but just as he approached the climax two of his dogs erupted into a ferocious fight.

Hild screamed and, grabbing them by the wrists, snatched Cynfeddw and Medwyl from danger. We all sprung to our feet in alarm while the dogs, clinched in a terrifying ball of hatred, snarled and growled about the floor.

Hunter, Cadafael's favourite had the other by the throat, the smaller dog yelping, grey tufts of fur flying. A pandemonium of screaming issued from the children and their father stood up and hurled a stool into the melee.

'Get away,' he yelled, his face empurpled. He strode across the furs to apply his boot to the problem until Hunter slunk away. The younger dog fled beneath a table and began to lick her wounds, keeping a wary, bloodshot eye on her opponent. While the dust settled the women took a little time to smooth their ruffled feathers and the children continued to sob until Cadafael resumed his seat and held out his arms.

'Come,' he jerked his head. 'Come, sit on my knee.'

Cynfeddw cuffed his tears and clambered onto his father's lap, followed by Medwyl who snuggled to his chest and grasped the collar of his tunic for security.

'Anyway, where was I? Oh, yes. I was very afraid but I couldn't show it or my father would have been angry. I held my spear aloft and stood my ground as the giant beast hurtled through the wood toward me…'

My mind wandered. The faces of my companions, only half visible in the poor light, were absorbed in Cadafael's story but I felt as restless as the hunting dogs. It was so long since I had felt the sun on my face. I closed my eyes and, trying to ignore the thick cloying air of the hall, I remembered the joy of standing on the hilltop with the summer wind stirring my hair, the tang of the sea tickling my nose.

Winter was hard but it was churlish of me to mind it when I had warmth and food in plenty for there were many who perished for lack of it. I pulled my wrap close, stretching my toes to the fire and Gwarw frowned at me, silently warning me of the risk of chill blains. I ignored her and vowed that, the very next time the sun poked his head from beneath the gloom, I would take the children for a long, brisk walk.

It was a week or more before the opportunity presented itself. I felt the change in the weather before I opened my eyes. A bright sword of daylight cut like a blade through the dim chamber. I pulled myself onto my pillows and inhaled a lungful of frigid air. It was much colder. Gwarw, with an old fur clutched about her shoulders, came limping into the room with my bearskin cloak over one arm.

'You will need this today, even in here.' She laid the cloak on the bed and wiped a drip of snot from the end of her nose. 'It's taken a turn for the worse out there.'

I slid from the bed to peer between the shutters. A thick layer of snow covered the enclosure, the roofs of the buildings were ennobled somehow by the pristine shroud. I wrapped my arms about my shoulders and shivered.

'Get your slippers on, Heledd. What are you thinking of? And your cloak too, look.'

She held out the garment and I shrugged into it gratefully and huddled before the fire while she brought me a bowl of porrage.

'We will go out today.' I announced. 'Tell Hild to dress the children extra warmly, it's time we got some fresh air.'

As I spoke Ffreur skipped, unannounced into my chamber.

'Oh Heledd, isn't it lovely? Shall we go for a walk? The children will love the snow, they haven't seen it before, have they?'

I put down my bowl. 'I was just telling Gwarw to wrap them up warm. Hedyn can stay with one of the women.' The cold air made Ffreur's face pinker than ever. She threw back the hood of her cloak and joined me at the hearth.

'I will wait here at the flames while you dress.'

At first the children did not know what to make of the altered landscape as we crossed the slushy mud of the enclosure and emerged onto the hillside. They tiptoed warily through the crisp drifts until Ffreur scooped up a handful and threw it at Cynfeddw.

It hit him square in the chest and for a moment he stood amazed, watching it cascade down his cloak. Then, suddenly understanding the game, a gleeful glint entered his eye and he bent down, filled his fist with snow and returned fire. I did not join in the fun but watched them as they ran, ducking and dodging the missiles, toward the bottom of the hill.

The mere was a sheet of blue ice, stretching across the valley, and the wild fowl, deprived of food, huddled together for safety in the centre, their heads tucked down into their bodies. The contrast of the white world against the dark skies was an invigorating sight and for once I was glad to be alive.

I took deep breaths, expelling the stale air, the cold fresh stuff hitting my lungs and making me cough.

The children ran ahead across the meadow, intrigued by the icy puddles. Cynfeddw, his hood thrown back, bent over for a closer look.

'The water is hard,' he announced. 'I can stand on it, look.'

He jumped up and down for good measure and grinned up at us, his face flushed with discovery. As he sped ahead I smiled and moved on toward the jetty, scanning the far shore with dazzled eyes. There were no boats today, the change in the weather having prevented any small craft from sailing. In such weather even the hardiest of traders stayed at home.

The wooden planks were slippery underfoot and, leaving my ladies in a huddle in the meadow, I approached the edge with caution and stood looking across the sparkling expanse of ice. It glistened like a huge jewel, the sunshine discovering a myriad of subtle colours, the protruding reeds embellished with tiny miracles of frost.

Hugging my fur close and dipping my red nose into the warmth of my collar I acknowledged to myself that perhaps it was time we returned to the llys before we all grew too chilled. The weather was so extraordinarily cold that it would not do to keep the children out very much longer. With a last look I turned away, seeking the children and what I saw made me freeze like stone.

Cynfeddw, having escaped the scrutiny of his nurse, was standing on the thin ice at the edge of the mere, close by the jetty.

'Look, Mother, I am walking on the water.' He glided away from the edge. For a few precious moments I could not catch my breath. I could not speak.

'Cynfeddw,' my voice rasped. 'Keep very still. Do not move. It isn't safe.'

His face was red, his eyes gleaming, the picture of health but I knew that he stood just inches from death. Somehow I found myself kneeling at the very edge of the jetty. I stretched out a hand, forced a smile, trying to keep my voice calm so as not to panic him.

'Take my hand, Cynfeddw, I will pull you up.' He looked over to Hild and Ffreur who were playing snowballs with Medwyl.

'I don't want to,' he pouted. 'It's fun.'

I licked my lips, fighting for composure. 'It is dangerous, child, come take my hand.'

He folded his arms and his lips tightened and I recognised the familiar flash of temper in his eye. He was like me, ill-natured and disobedient. I sensed his action before he made it. 'No!' My cry was hoarse with pent up terror but he ignored me, and with a look that bid me go to the devil, he stamped his foot.

My scream echoed across the valley. I lunged for his hand just as the ice gave way and the water took him. I did not let go but the weight of him was pulling me after. I leaned perilously over the jetty, my knees breaking, my stomach screaming with the effort not to fall in. His eyes were wide, his mouth squared with horror. For a brief moment I knew that if I held on to him we would both be lost, but he was my son, how could I let him go?

I held on, my knees slipping on the rough planking, my skirts already sodden. He clung to my arm, scrabbled at my dangling braids, his frozen fingers too stiff to grip properly. For the briefest of moments I knew we faced the end and, at the moment of our death, I was at last consumed with love for him, my first born.

And then the water, too cold for description, engulfed us both. Shocked senseless, I could not breathe but somehow I managed to hold onto him, feeling him kick, trying to free himself, the water surging in my ears, numbing cold slowing my movement. We floundered together, fighting for the surface but I could not think, could not work my limbs properly, the weight of the bearskin was pulling me down. I tasted muddy water, felt the spectral fingers of the reeds entwine about my ankles. And I knew we would die.

And then, a great surge in the water and strong hands beneath my armpits, pulling me upward. I clung to my son as we were dragged to the surface and emerged into the frigid over-world, gulping mouthfuls of delicious air.

I was flung onto the jetty, the hard boards crashing against my skull. I heard women crying, the rasping breath of my son, the shrill panic of Medwyl. I opened my eyes and saw feet, the muddy hem of Ffreur's skirts and Cadafael's boots.

Someone grabbed me beneath the arms, hauled me onto a horse and I found myself cradled against Cadafael's chest. Barely conscious, I clung to him, with one arm wrapped about Cynfeddw, his head lolling lifeless against my breast as Cadafael lashed his horse mercilessly, sending it surging forward.

My head rasped against his mailed chest as the horse scrabbled over the icy shale, fighting a desperate way to the top. The bitter wind penetrated my sodden garments so completely I might as well have been naked. My teeth clashed together but I clung to Cadafael, my husband. The man who suddenly represented life itself.

By the time we thundered through the gates and into the enclosure I was so cold I could barely discern what was happening. I glanced down at my son who lay in my arms his face a deathly blue, his eyes closed, lips colourless. I knew he was dead but there was no time to weep.

Cadafael half dragged me into my chamber and, dumping me on the bed, threw a fur over me. I huddled beneath it, in a nightmare of shivering, my hair dripping, watching helplessly as he stripped the clothes from our son and wrapped his skinny body in a bed fur. Yelling for a servant to stoke the fires, he began to rub my boy's limbs. He showed little sign of life, his limp body and senseless face like that of a ghost. I had never properly loved him. I had resented him for not being Osian's and now I hated myself for my blindness. Panic was not far away and, as it surged upward into my throat again, I whimpered.

Cadafael glanced at me.

'He lives,' he said briefly and turned back to his work. I watched in shaking silence, noting his determination and realising through the glacial numbness of my mind just how very much he loved our son.

After a very long while Cynfeddw stirred, coughed and opened his eyes, just a slit, but he did not recognise his father. I held my breath. Cadafael stopped rubbing and sat up, held a cup of warmed mead to his lips. The child sputtered but his father bade him drink some more and he obeyed. Cadafael pulled the fur firmly up to the boy's chin and looked toward me. By this time I was shivering so hard that my teeth chattered audibly and, satisfied that his son would live, Cadafael left the hearth and came toward the bed.

I trembled as he stripped away my layers of clothing and dropped them one by one into a heap on the floor. When I was quite naked, he wrapped me in a bed fur and as he had done for Cynfeddw, slid his hands beneath it and began to rub my body. His hands moved quickly and roughly across my skin, bringing an agonisingly slow return of feeling. When he had rubbed me all over he took a bare foot, his calloused hands moving up my calf, then over my knees until he worked his way to my thigh. Painfully, the blood began to return and my skin, crinkled and blue, burning beneath his touch.

The water ran from my hair, trickling across my breasts, pooling in the bowl of my belly and all the time I wept pathetically, like a child until, slowly I began to feel a little warmer and realised that perhaps I'd not die after all.

At length he stood up, handed me a cup of mead and turned back to his son but Cynfeddw, wrapped in his fur and overcome by the heat of the fire and the strong spirits he had drunk, had fallen asleep. There was some colour in his cheeks now. Cadafael turned back to me and I saw the glimmer of relief. He plonked himself on the edge of my bed and took my cup, drank from it, exhaustion etched upon his face.

'I think you will both live, Madam.'

I put out a hand to thank him and found his jerkin soaking. 'Cadafael! You are drenched.'

I scrambled up and began to help him undo his lacings, shrunk by the water and impossible for my frozen fingers. In the end he took his dagger and cut himself free and I stripped away his clothes. Then he wrapped himself in a fur and crept with me beneath the bed covers.

We clung together, desperate for each other's warmth and soon, in the encroaching glow of our shared heat, locked in one another's arms, we slept while, outside, the storm blew up afresh.

PART FOUR
FFREUR'S REFRAIN

Fair Ffreur! there are brothers who cherish thee,
And who have not sprung from the ungenerous;
They are men who cherish no timidity.

654-5

Hedyn pulled earnestly at my nipple, a frown on his face, one pink hand curled possessively on the mound of my breast. He was about four moons old and had totally captured my heart. In the centre of the room the fire roared, a tray of chestnuts cooking in the embers. It was the end of a long afternoon. At the hearth Ffreur plucked at a lyre and sang, her voice husky with emotion. I knew her courses had flowed again that morning and wondered how I could cheer her.

    We had been incarcerated for weeks due to the heavy snow and, one by one, we had all succumbed to colds. From the passage came the sound of Cynfeddw's voice followed by the cajoling tones of his nurse then the door opened, a gust of chill air blew in and the chamber erupted with life. Cynfeddw, well-recovered from his dip in the icy mere, issued a perfunctory bow.

    'Good day, Mother,' he said and, ignoring his brother, took his place on a cushion before the fire. Medwyl bobbed a curtsey and smiled, her fat cheeks liberally smeared with drying snot. She climbed on the stool and peered over my shoulder to look at the baby.

'Gwarw,' I said, 'get her down. I don't want the babe getting a cold.' The child backed away, guided by the old woman's hand and sat beside Cynfeddw.

'I like the babby,' she announced, earning herself a scowl from my eldest son.

'I don't,' he said and pushed his playmate from her cushion.

'Of course you do,' I snapped. 'Wait until he is grown and can join in the fun, you will like him better then.' Cynfeddw set his jaw and I thrust away the undeniable fact that he was a replica of me and told myself instead that he was exactly like his father.

'No, I won't. Babies are stupid and I think that one is a changeling, why else should his hair be red.'

My heart gave a little leap of fear and I wondered who had been gossiping for his words were not those of a child.

'How silly,' I gave him a doting smile. 'Your grandmother was red-headed. Hedyn takes after her, that is all.'

He wiped his nose on his sleeve and looked at the slimy trail left there.

'Angharad said he is a changeling. She said that dark-headed parents give birth to dark-headed babies. The fairies took your real son away and left that one instead.'

'Perhaps Angharad needs to feel the cut of my whip.'

Ffreur put down her harp and came closer to the fire, kneeling on the cushions with the children.

'I was talking to Twm this morning, you know young Twm from the cooking hall? Well, he told me that the kitchen cat has six new-born kittens. Shall we visit them after prayers?'

I shot her a thankful glance and disengaging Hedyn's mouth from my nipple, sat him like a small sack on my lap while I rubbed his back. He let out a loud burp and a trail of milk trickled down his chin. Cynfeddw and Medyl dissolved into laughter, making a quiver of amusement tug at the corners of my own mouth, but I sobered quickly and offered Hedyn my other breast.

'Can I have a kitten, Mother, one of my own to keep in my sleeping place?' Now Cynfeddw was all smiles, cajoling and sweet, but I refused to be pacified.

'We will have to see how good you are; how well you do at your studies; how polite you are to me; how nice you are to your brother.'

Deflated, he flopped back on the cushion and then, catching sight of the chestnuts, reached out to take one.

'Ow!'

The chamber flew into disarray as Ffreur snatched his hand from the hearth and doused it with ale, drenching both his hand and the arm of his tunic. He sat dripping, his mouth open in a great wail of self-pity and Medwyl, seeing his anguish, immediately joined in. I leaned forward, dislodging Hedyn from my nipple who, vexed at the loss, added his own screams to the racket. And on to this chaotic scene came Cadafael.

'Father.' Cynfeddw held out his arms, a picture of grief and the King swept the boy into his arms, hugging him while Medwyl leapt onto his foot and clung to his leg. Cadafael's hounds began to bark and one of them swept a tray of drinks from the table with his great tail.

My feelings for Cynfeddw had never been strong and from the very beginning he had been his father's son. Since I nearly lost him I had hoped I would be more tolerant toward him but he irritated me enormously and as for Medwyl, well, I began to wonder why I put up with either her or her dratted mother. Something inside me snapped.

'Oh, for Frith's sake.' I stood up, dumped Hedyn onto Gwarw's lap and disappeared into my sleeping place where, safe behind the curtain, I put my hands to my head and slumped onto the bed. There was never any peace. I longed to be left alone, to get to know my new son, to listen to music, to dream of Osian. I wanted contentment and most of all, to stop feeling so very alone. Even though I was constantly surrounded by people; family, servants and children, the solitude was unbearable. Tears of self-pity dripped upon my fingers.

I wiped my eyes with the heels of my hand, blew my nose and took a deep, ragged breath. I should go back to the company but I could hear Cadafael and Ffreur consoling the children, and Gwarw was pacing the floor with the babe, singing gently. They seemed to be managing without me.

Why could I not like them? Why did they exasperate me so? Was domesticity always like this? After a time it went quiet. I heard the door close and someone stoking the fire, and then a soft footstep and the curtain parted.

Cadafael poked his head through the gap but did not enter until I gave him leave with a jerk of my head. He came closer and sat beside me on the bed. 'Ffreur tells me you have been out of sorts.' He fiddled with the tassel on his sword belt, and when I did not answer continued, 'would you like a break? A journey to your brother's court perhaps?'

My neck snapped upward. His genuine concern shamed me and guilt twisted in my gut. If I returned to Cynddylan's Hall I would see Osian again. I could show him his son. Tears stung my eyes, I longed to agree but I knew what I had to do.

I shook my head. 'Hedyn is too young to travel yet, but later maybe, when he is weaned.'

Cadafael took my hand, tiny in his huge, brown one. 'You could wean him early and find a wet nurse, as you did for Cynfeddw.'

My hand was growing warmer within his. He stroked the back of it, watching my skin ripple beneath his touch. I'd not known him so tender before and when he brought my fingers to his lips and kept it there, I was surprised to feel a little spark of desire … or something.

I sat unmoving while he turned the palm upward and kissed it, his tongue making my heart leap and a squirm of desire wriggle to the pit of my stomach. Feeling like an adulterer for not stopping him I watched as, without a word, he worked his way to my inner elbow, tracing circles on my skin, then further to my shoulder, stopping to push back my sleeve and kiss each freckle.

It was like a dream. He had never been so tender. I was entranced by his head dark against my white skin and when he transferred his lips to my neck, his beard softly tickling, I leant my head back and closed my eyes, gasping when his hand slipped into my open bodice.

A little groan escaped me and thus encouraged, he massaged my nipple making the milk flow, my breasts groan with wanting, and when he pushed me gently back onto the pillow and covered my mouth with his, for the first time I did not want him to stop.

Two

Immediately afterwards I was consumed with guilt. In willingly sleeping with my husband I had betrayed Osian. I wished to be alone so that I could give in to my shame but Cadafael lingered. Propping himself on pillows, he pulled me close and cradled my head upon his naked chest and fiddled with a tress of my hair that lay in tangles around us. When he did speak his words astounded me. 'Something happened to me while I was away ... I, I won't go into detail but it made me see that the troubles between us are of my own making. If I can, Heledd, I would like to put things right.'

The memory of the last hour was still vivid and, not knowing how to answer, I flushed scarlet and murmured something about him having made a good start already.

But I could not banish Osian's face. It kept intruding, floating in my mind's eye, taunting me with guilt and spoiling the pleasure of the moment. Cadafael continued to speak.

'Since we were wed I have watched Iestyn and Ffreur with no little envy but I could never seem to reach you. Even in the beginning, I wanted to laugh and joke with you like Ffreur and Iestyn do but I have ... had ... little knowledge of women beyond the technicalities. I have only known whores and such and I did not know where to start with you. In the bedchamber, you were there in the bed, yet unreachable like one of those Roman statues, beautiful and mine yet far, far removed. I did not know what to do with you or how to begin to soften the stone.'

He stroked the curve of my bosom, his breath hot in my hair. I fidgeted my legs, the heat rising again. Beneath my ear his heart was beating fast, I watched the rise and fall of his furry stomach, the trail of dark hair leading to the bulge of his groin beneath the sheet. I was so tired of solitude. So tired of misery. I took a deep breath.

'It is not too late, is it? Perhaps we should begin again, my lord.'

His arm tightened about my shoulder, flattening my breasts against his body. I did not love him but something within me was stirring. It was as if I'd been imprisoned in darkness and surprisingly it was Cadafael's hand that was reaching down to pull me up into the light.

He rolled me suddenly onto my back, our faces level, our eyes searching. Slowly his mouth spread into a lazy smile and he smoothed a strand of hair from my face.

'You are very beautiful, you know,' he said.

I blushed like a virgin and knew not what to say, so I said nothing. Instead, I pushed Osian's image away and with a trembling finger, traced the line of Cadafael's jaw and the curve of his nose before raising my mouth to his.

Three

Ffreur was both curious and insistent in her questioning. 'Something has happened between you,' she said, barring my path so I could not pass. 'What has changed? Tell me.' Her face was pleased and excited. 'Iestyn and I could not believe the two of you the other night behaving like a pair of doves. I would know the secret, sister, that I might reinvigorate my own husband.'

I laughed aloud at that for Iestyn was still as smitten with her as the first day he saw her. Most men would have put away a barren wife but he never showed, either by word or action, that he bore any resentment. How I wished she could bear a child and complete their happiness. Linking her arm in mine, I walked with her across the enclosure.

'I have done nothing. He came back from the last campaign changed; that is all. I suspect there is another woman behind it but I can't say I mind.' Then, suddenly attacked by another wave of guilt at my previous infidelity, I averted my eyes and as if she had read my thoughts, she pulled me on to a wooden bench.

'What about your feelings for the singer, Osian, have they faded?'

'I don't know, Ffreur, when I think of him, my feelings are gentle but I must confess that these days my thoughts do not dwell on him as they once did. There is barely time, my husband is very demanding.'

I raised my brows coyly and she laughed and patted my knee,

'That is a good thing. A woman's thoughts should be with her husband. You are a Queen, the mother of future Kings, your husband is a great warrior and your life is good. That is as it should be. I am happy for you. It has been a long time coming.'

Indeed, her eyes were flooded with happiness and I could not help but embrace her. She was right. I did feel better and in my contentment I found it was easier to behave as nobly as my mother would have wanted. I was growing kind and generous, winning the good favour of my servants. At last I was a good Queen to Cadafael and the people of Gwynedd.

I looked at Ffreur. 'And you, Sister, is life good for you too?'

She maintained her smile but I felt her sadness. She gave a little sigh.

'I am happy, but for one thing,' she said, 'and I don't have to tell you what that is.' Her chin drooped but she fought to maintain her cheerfulness. In my newfound happiness I wished everyone about me to be as content as I. I grabbed her wrist, hard.

'Ffreur,' her tear-washed eyes flew up to mine. 'Come with me to Ceri, she will help you, I know she can. Look how she helped at my birthing. I would be dead now were it not for her.'

Ffreur snatched away her hand. 'Oh, no, Heledd, I cannot. Ceri is a well-meaning woman but she is misguided, her methods go against God's teaching.' Her head swept to and fro and confronted with such stubbornness, anger stabbed me.

'If your God was so good he'd have given you a child. I don't know a woman on this earth more worthy of motherhood than you.'

'It is something I must learn to bear, Heledd. If it is God's plan for me then I can only accept it.'

I remembered Ffreur in the circle of firelight at my birthing, joining in with the others to chant an incantation against my pain. Twice she had put aside her faith for my sake so, just maybe, she would do so again, not for herself perhaps, but for someone she loved. The devil in me stirred.

'What of Iestyn?' I tempted. 'How can you watch his suffering? Have you not seen his pain when Cynfeddw climbs upon his knee? He longs for a child, Ffreur, and all it would cost you is one visit to Ceri and I swear you'd be pregnant by the month's end.'

I heard a short intake of breath, felt her hand, cold upon my own. Her voice was barely audible when she answered.

'I will think on it, Heledd. I will search my soul and listen for God's answer.' When she moved away I sat back upon the bench with a satisfied smile for I knew I had won, and considered it a well-fought victory.

I followed her to the ladies bower where Gwarw was dandling Hedyn on her knee, humming a tune, tempting him to smile. He was sparing of them as yet but every so often he would open his milky mouth and bestow a beam of sunshine upon whoever nursed him. I sat myself in my usual chair and all I could see of him was a fuzz of red hair above his bands. Gwarw leaned over him, doting and daft.

The door opened and Cadafael strode in. He threw his wolf's pelt cloak upon a stool and sent me a cheery greeting before lifting Hedyn from Gwarw's arms. She was suffering with her feet again but tottered off to fetch refreshments from the ante-chamber. Cadafael held my son up to the light. 'Good Lord, but he is growing fast. What are you feeding him; pork?' He offered a finger and I saw Hedyn grab it and try to stuff it into his mouth. Cadafael sauntered about the chamber with the child nestled in the crook of his arm. 'There is news, wife.' I could see by his playful expression that his news was good.

'Is Oswiu dead?' I asked, evoking a shout of laughter.

'That would be good news indeed, my love. No, 'tis family news, word that will please you.'

I was at a loss to guess and held out my empty hands. 'Oh, I don't know! Come, Cadafael, tell me.' I got up and hung on his free arm. 'Please?'

When I put on my best pout he could not resist me and, sliding his free arm about my waist, he drew me closer. 'Your brother, Cynddylan, is taking a wife and invites us to his hall in celebration.'

Ffreur and I exchanged our delight but even as we embraced, I felt a shiver of doubt at returning to Pengwern and seeing Osian again. What on earth would I say to him?

Cynfeddw crawled about the floor with his father's cloak over his head.

'Grrrrr,' he cried. 'Beware, I am a fearsome wolf.' Medwyl pretending terror, jumped screaming, onto a stool.

With Cadafael's arm warm about my waist we watched the antics of our family, their merriment contagious and when Gwarw came waddling back into the room she joined in the fun.

'Mercy me!' she cried. 'A great wolf is in the chamber. Help us, help us!' Then collapsing on to her stool she signalled for the slave to place the tray upon the table.

For the first time I became aware of Angharad's presence. She plonked the tray down noisily, casting a quick eye over the domestic chaos then, after bobbing briefly to Cadafael, she shot me a look of pure venom.

She would have slammed the door had she dared.

Four

'It is almost dark.' I said to Ffreur who, wrapped in her cloak sat huddled in the corner. 'We shall go now.'

We crept from the bower, not wanting to be seen and I led her by a surreptitious route out onto the hillside. Far below the moon glimmered on the mere and, in the distance, the river slithered like a silver snake toward the sea. Wrapping our cloaks tight against the chilly wind, we began to descend the hill. To guard against the evils of witchcraft Ffreur wore a posy of yellow flowers and she clung to my arm, afraid of the dark and the evil things that lurked in the covert.

'Don't worry, it is safe,' I assured her. 'I have passed this way many a time.' She flashed me a tense smile before disappearing once more beneath her hood.

We hurried on through deepest dark until we spied a tiny light that signalled Ceri's hut was near. When she saw it Ffreur hesitated but I pulled her on.

'You can't go back now. Just think of your child.' She bit her lip and I watched her wrestle frantically with her conscience. I knew she wanted to run back to the brightly lit hall but, just at that moment, the door opened and Ceri beckoned us in.

It was warm, the fire roared and a cauldron of cawl hung over the flames filling the room with the aroma of home and well-being. Ffreur sat on a stool and threw back her hood, her hair gleaming bright in the gloom. We sipped gratefully at a cup of Ceri's warming brew as she seated herself before us.

'Now, My Queen, what can I do for you? 'Tis another bairn you carry, I see.' My hand flew instinctively to my womb and I glanced at Ffreur who turned her head toward the hearth. I decided to ignore the welcome news.

'It is not for me I come, Ceri, but my sister, Ffreur.'

Ceri worked her gums for a while, looking along her crooked nose at my little sister who sat like a nun in a house of demons. The old woman nodded slowly. 'Barren, are you?' she asked.

Ffreur nodded.

'Does your husband service you well?'

Ffreur flushed and, as if suddenly making up her mind, looked Ceri full in the face. 'We have done everything to make a child. I crave one, Ceri, for my husband's sake … more than my own.'

With a mirthless sound Ceri motioned her to lay down upon the bed for examination and Ffreur, her tunic raised and her knees splayed, fixed her frantic gaze on me while Ceri prodded and poked at her most private places. My little sister, shamed and humiliated, dug her teeth into her lip, turning it white and I saw a tear roll onto the pillow. My heart turned over with love for her and to spare her blushes, I looked about the dim interior until at last Ceri stood up and Ffreur was able to pull down her skirts.

Ceri lowered herself onto a stool. 'I can find nothing wrong with you. I think we just need to give nature a little help.' She leered a smile and I began to feel better but Ffreur's nod was miserable. Her hands were clasped tightly in her lap when Ceri leaned forward and lowered her voice.

'What we need to do is this.'

Five

As she instructed we waited until the waxing of the moon before we visited Ceri again. The night was colder than before for it was almost a whole month closer to winter than our last visit. I had begun to vomit in the mornings and my breasts strained taught and tender against my garments. Cadafael had been busy, plotting war with his brother so I had not found the right time to tell him that our loving had made fruit.

'I can't believe we are going through with this.' Ffreur's trembling hands clutched my arm as we crept from the llys. At Ceri's direction we were both naked beneath our cloaks and Ffreur was anxious that someone would see us.

'Hush, do not tremble so.' I placed a hand over hers and found it as cold as stone. 'All will be well, I trust Ceri. She knows her art.'

Ffreur shuddered. She did not share my faith and I knew it was only love for Iestyn and desperation to give him a child that drove her on. We pushed on through the shadows, glad when the twinkling of Ceri's candle showed through the trees. She was waiting at the end of the path and, raising a finger to her lips, beckoned us deeper into the wood.

The ground was littered with fallen leaves and twigs that cracked and snapped beneath our feet. Ffreur jumped at every sound; small beasts scurrying through the undergrowth; nocturnal hunters on the prowl while above us the air shivered with the wings of flitter-mice and an owl called loudly from nearby. We stopped in our tracks to watch as it passed silently, like a spirit, above our heads.

'Come along,' Ceri urged and we followed her downhill, through the wood toward a rocky spring where the tree trunks gleamed pale in the moonlight. 'Take off your cloaks,' she ordered and I threw mine off while Ffreur, more slowly, let her own slither to the floor so that it lay like a puddle where it fell.

Her waist length hair gleamed silver-blonde and I followed in the tracks of her muddy feet to a pool, fed by a cataract that filtered through the hillside.

'Get in,' Ceri instructed. 'Immerse yourselves.'

The water was cold. We opened our mouths and gasped as it covered our bellies and lapped against our breasts. When Ceri threw off her own rags and waded toward us we did not laugh. She walked upright, somehow ennobled by the strange patterns painted upon the swaying remnants of her body. She emanated an unworldly power, the mystery of the night endowing her with a kind of sacred beauty.

She glided through the water, her face raised to the moon, her eyes rolled backwards and strange words upon her lips. Then she lifted her arms and placed a hand on each of our heads. I cannot recall the words that she made over us. All I remember is my skin trembling at her touch and Ffreur's wide terrified eyes shining from the dark.

The chanting ceased and Ceri suddenly plunged us both beneath the surface of the pool and held us there with surprising strength. Her hand was heavy. I could not breathe. My lungs began to fill with water and, for a horrified moment, I thought she meant to drown us.

I began to fight, a great gurgling filling my ears as I kicked out, gulping mouthfuls of brackish water. Ffreur and I broke the surface at the same time. Gasping, we clung together, coughing and fighting to refill our lungs with blessed air.

Ceri remained entranced, her eyeballs white, she continued her muttering, stroking a hand over my belly before cupping it over Ffreur's. She pressed our bodies together and instinctively we embraced. I felt the old woman's hand on the base of my spine, as though she sought to mould us, one to the other. My sister's body was like a child's. She was covered with goose pimples, her tiny breasts jutting forward, the pink tips erect. My own was round, my motherly breasts large and blue-veined with fat brown nipples.

And, quite suddenly, it became clear to me that, in some mystical manner Ceri was sharing my own fertility with my sister. I clutched Ffreur closer, pressing my breasts into hers, wrapping my legs about her. She gasped, her wet hair clinging to my arms, her lashes separated into stars. The wind rose and howled through the clattering branches above our head and Ffreur shook with fear at the screaming powers that surged around us. I laughed aloud, triumphant in my understanding.

Ceri's voice grew louder, more authoritative, and at her command our psyches mingled, our souls touched. Ffreur and I became like a serpent on a carving, its tail held fast in its own throat, there was no telling where she ended and I began. Throwing back my head I gave in to a kind of ecstasy and revelled with the spirits that danced around us in the watery glade.

Much later, when the wind had dropped and the darkness grown less intense we climbed, dripping, from the water and wrapped ourselves gladly in our cloaks. Ffreur's lips were tinged blue and water ran from the ends of her hair in rivulets but she would not meet my eye. Embarrassed at the passion that had passed between us, we pulled on our boots and followed Ceri back through the lightening wood. We hurried up the path to the llys and at the door of the women's bower we said goodnight and passed into our separate chambers, our separate lives.

Gwarw had waited up for me, she grumbled as she grabbed a drying cloth and began to rub my hair. 'What have you been up to now, child? Look at your hair dripping all over your mantle, are you mad to wet yourself all over at his time of year?'

I laughed gently at her mithering. I was tired but happy with the knowledge that some of the fertility that lay curled in my womb had been shared with Ffreur. I grinned as if I were moon-mazed, gladly bearing her ministrations and her nagging before climbing among the furs and sleeping until noon.

Six

Cadafael held out his arms and I went into them happily. 'A daughter, this time, I hope.' He planted a kiss on my head and squeezed me and, although the joy I felt was not the ecstatic bliss I had shared with Osian, it was warm and easy.

'I would like a daughter,' I confessed, imagining a tiny version of myself, or better still, of Ffreur. 'The child should be here by mid- summer, in time for Cynddylan's wedding, a double celebration.'

He yawned and stretched. 'Come, wife, let us to our bed. I am tired and the chamber is growing chill.'

Over the last months he had spent more nights in my chamber than not and I hoped he had ceased to visit Angharad. I had certainly stopped providing her with bribes to keep him from me. I found to my surprise that I enjoyed his company. Now that I was no longer pushing him away, looking for reasons not to share his bed, we were growing closer and it was not just at nightfall that I looked for his presence.

I lay on his chest watching the flickering light on the chamber wall, enjoying the way he stroked my upper arm with a lazy hand.

'My brother tells me Ffreur has quickened at last.' His words evoked that strange night in the glade when Ceri had made Freur's child partly my own. Joy in the knowledge unfurled in my belly.

'It is wonderful, isn't it? I have never seen a woman so happy in her vomit.' Our laughter murmured in the dark.

He shifted his position. 'Good night, Heledd.' His lips were warm, his beard tickling and when he made to move away, I increased the pressure of my mouth slightly and clung to his jerkin, prolonging the kiss. I was rewarded instantly when he threw off his lethargy, rolled me on my back to love me one more time.

It was dark when I awoke and my limbs were cramped. I longed to stretch them but I did not move for his arms were still tight about me. Feeling safe and more cherished than ever in my life before, I lay unmoving, listening to the steady rhythm of his heart.

In the morning after we had made love again, he threw back the covers and, evading my clutching hands, backed playfully from the bed.

'Leave me, woman, there are things a King must do. You could kill me with too much loving.'

I pouted, drawing the sheet to my chin and watching him with a shameless gleam of lust in my eye. He saw me leering and pretending embarrassment, shielded his loins from my gaze. 'I said later, Madam.' He was as coy as Ffreur, his play acting making me scream with laughter. I threw a cushion at him before rolling onto my belly and stretching my limbs down to the bottom of the bed.

'Go your way, Husband,' I teased, pretending indifference. 'At least I have a fair share of the mattress now. I may lie abed 'til supper time.'

'That wouldn't surprise me in the least,' he quipped as he opened the door. 'At least I shall know where to find you.'

My smile lingered long after he had gone, I snuggled into the sheets reliving the dark secrets of the night, relishing the scent of him on the pillows, looking forward to nightfall.

Seven

The small bulge of Ffreur's stomach thrilled me as much as if it had been my own child she carried. Every day we sat in the ladies bower fashioning small garments and planning the future. Our babies would be born just weeks apart and we knew their bond would be strong, like our own.

'What will you call him?' I asked.

She put down her spindle, her cheeks pink with pleasure. 'Iestyn likes the name Ianto, and I am happy to let him choose.' Picking up her work again she continued to ply her thread. Beside her, I leaned closer to my work.

'What if it should be a girl?'

She stopped again. 'I don't think it will be, although I won't mind, but I think Iestyn would prefer a boy, all men want a son, don't they? If it were a girl, I think I would have to call her Heledd.'

I raised my eyes, feigning humour when really I was very touched.

'Another one? May the gods preserve us!'

She laughed, her veil falling across her face as she ducked her head to her work again. I relished the gentle smile that played on her face all the time these days. She hugged the future to herself, in love with the child she carried. We continued in silence while the flames crackled in the hearth and the everyday sounds of the llys floated in through the door. Then she spoke again, surprising me with her question.

'Heledd, do you ever think of Mother?'

'Of course I do, don't you?'

'Yes, often. She was such a lovely, gentle woman. I wish she were here, I could do with her guidance.'

I put my own sewing aside, leaned back in my chair and clasped my hands across the expanse of my belly. 'Don't worry, everything will be fine, Ffreur. You will be safe in Ceri's care, just as I was. And remember your God will be watching over you.'

She did not reply at once and just then, Hild and the children tumbled into the room after a jaunt to the river. Cynfeddw tugged at my skirt, Medwyl at his side, to show me a treasure they had discovered on the hillside and above their high-pitched clamour I thought I heard Ffreur whisper, 'Will he?'

While I grew cumbersome, my belly rivalling the hills of Gwynedd, Ffreur remained petite, the only change being the gentle rise of her belly and the swelling of her breasts. She had no trouble rising from her chair as I did and her step remained light and dainty.

Cadafael teased me, grabbing my wrist and hauling me from my seat as though he were a fisherman fighting to land a great sea cow. But at night, in the privacy of our curtained bed, he revelled in my fruitfulness, stroking the rise of my womb and my engorged breasts, squeezing tiny drops of milk from my nipples.

'Ah, wife,' he murmured between kisses. 'You are magnificent.' And when he took me he was gentle, holding himself back, cherishing the babe I nurtured. He had fulfilled his duty. I was already pregnant and he had no need to visit me. He could, at any time, have gone to Angharad or some other whore but he came to me, because he wanted to and I was glad.

Our bed became like a great buoyant ship, floating upon a sea of laughter. I had never been so content and wished it would never end. My times with Osian had always been tainted by the fear of discovery but this newfound love was legitimate, and relaxed ... and real.

Even in the depths of my present misery those times can still make me smile for they are the most precious I have shared with anyone. For the first time in my life I was properly happy ... for the only time.

But no days are entirely without cloud and soon the threat of war loomed large again. I stood a little apart from the company as the men prepared to ride out once more. Cadafael had expected no more trouble after putting down Cadwaladr and sending him to exile but some of his former supporters were rabble rousing. This time Cadafael was determined to silence them once and for all.

Although I had never worried before when he rode off on a campaign, this time I felt great pain at his leaving and a gnawing, unacknowledged fear that, perhaps, he would not return. Although I did not let one syllable of panic pass my lips, it was impossible to stop my fearful tears from falling. My voice was trapped in my throat, my chin nobbled with grief as I watched him prepare to leave me. Irrational as it was I wanted to claw him back, beg him to stay, or dress myself in my page's clothes and ride off with him. But, when the time came for him to mount up, I was a coward and said nothing … as a queen should.

Cadafael was bellowing last minute orders at his men. Dressed in battle gear, his fearsome helmet beneath his arm, he bore little resemblance to the gentle man that shared the intimacy of my bed chamber. He caught sight of me cowering by the bower wall and our eyes met. The wind blew his hair across his face and he brushed it impatiently back, sending me a sorry smile before continuing to order his men. Then, his duty done, he turned and strode across the enclosure toward me, his smile regretful as he pushed me into the darkness of the bower, away from men's sight.

I craned my neck back, taking in the stark outline of his face. He reached out, touched my belly that strained against the fabric of my tunic, before raising his hand to my face.

'Take care, Heledd, of yourself and our little ones.'

To speak would have been to release all my fear, let him see my conviction that he would not be coming home. I nodded, swallowed the painful lump in my throat, and blinked away hot tears although more quickly followed, spilling down my cheeks. With blurred vision I watched as he swung into the saddle and, with a last glance in my direction, ordered the troop to ride out. I ran out into the dust thrown up by the horses' heels, I raised a hand but although I watched until the glint of his shield was just a tiny star in the distance, he did not turn around.

Then came the waiting. Weeks of worry, wondering if he still breathed; quivering at each messenger that scrambled up to the llys on a sweating pony. It was a wearisome spring with very few bright days interspersing the weeks of rain. I took to walking on the mountainside, thickly wrapped in furs, blaming my wet cheeks on the capricious wind. As I walked I sang to my unborn child, my only child conceived within the bounds of marital love. I stroked the outline of my belly and craved the man who had made it swell to come back safe.

At the end of April the weather turned on us when we least expected it, blasting us with a final rage of winter. As I stood looking out across the valley, willing the troop to appear on the road, the first grains of snow began to settle on my cloak. I dug my purple fists into my armpits and ducked my chin into my neck.

'Please come,' I whispered, as if I had the power to summon him from the clouds. 'Please.' I spoke the last plea aloud and jumped violently at a sound on the mountain shale behind me. When I spun round it was to find Hild had come to find me but was too timid to break into my reverie.

'Gwarw sent me.' She said apologetically, holding out an extra cloak. 'She said you are to come now and I'm to take no argument.'

I smiled weakly and surrendered to the summons. 'I will come,' I said, letting her fasten the cloak beneath my chin and raise the hood about my face. She took my hand and helped me down the hill toward home for the rocky path that I had climbed with little difficulty was now lethal with slush.

Inside, Gwarw thrust a steaming bowl of cawl into my hands and rubbed the dampness from my hair. 'You need to take more care,' she grumbled. 'If you have none for yourself then have some for your child. Look at you, your lips are blue. You should do as your sister does and stay by the fireside, you don't see her roaming the hillside do you?'

Ffreur looked up from her needle and flashed a conspiratorial smile. Gwarw had been nagging at us in this manner since we were children. I knew how to soothe her.

'You are right, Gwarw, and I have been foolish and headstrong. I swear I have no desire to leave the fireside for a long time. The wind has the bite of winter in it again and I so long for the summertime, when our babies will be here.'

We listened to the crackle of the flames and the wind creaking the roof timbers until a great shout came from outside and I jumped from my chair, spilling my broth down my tunic.

Ffreur abandoned her work, the skein of wool unwinding in the rushes, and we all rushed to the door in time to see Cadafael's squire slide from the back of his horse. Filthy and exhausted, he forgot the respect due to me and waved his arm back the way he had come.

'Your lord is coming, Lady. They are some four leagues or so behind me. Make ready for them, we have some wounded …'

I could see from his evasive eye that the tidings were ill and my heart lurched sickeningly against my ribs. I leapt forward, grabbed his arm. 'Who,' I cried. 'Who is wounded?'

His face worked for a while, his glance darting from me to my women who stood around me in a half circle. My heart beat loud and dull, making me nauseous. I could feel the bile rising in my throat. It was Cadafael, half-dead probably, either from injury or fatigue. From the churning of my stomach I knew I would be sick.

But he licked his lips, cleared his throat. 'Iestyn.'

The word rang out across the precinct and as I sent up a swift prayer to whoever was listening, I heard Ffreur scream a death knell, shattering our shared dream of peace.

While the women frantically prepared beds for the wounded, Gwarw and I did what we could to soothe Ffreur. She knelt in the slushy enclosure, the wet soaking through her skirts, her hand to her belly, grimacing in anguish. 'No,' she moaned over and over. 'Not Iestyn, please, not Iestyn.'

'Hush, Ffreur, hush, it may not be much. Breathe, my lover, calm yourself, think of the child.'

Gwarw rocked her back and forth, kneeling beside her in the mire, regardless of the cold biting into her old bones. I looked about me, the snow wetter now, angry clouds rolling in to swathe us all in rain. I peered into the distance but it was distorted by mist and cloud. I willed Cadafael to hurry.

My sister and Gwarw had not moved, Ffreur was beyond comfort. I tugged at Gwarw's shoulder, urged her to move, then I stood over my sister and forced myself to scream at her like a witch and, for the sake of herself and her precious child, shame her into action.

'Get up, Ffreur, what good will this do? Your man is stricken and in need of you and all you do is wallow in the mud. Get yourself up now and prepare to meet him with dignity. And think of your child, after all our trouble; will you sacrifice him for the sake of his father?'

She sniffed, hiccupped and looked up at me through her sodden veil. Beside her, Gwarw regarded me as if I were run mad and staggered to her feet.

'There's no need for that …' she began but Ffreur silenced her and held out a hand so that the old woman and I could help her to her feet and into the bower.

A warm drink and a change of clothes and, on the surface, we were almost our usual selves. The tip of Ffreur's nose was pink and her bloodshot eyes were like wounds in her deathly white face. She put a trembling hand to her head and tried to smile.

'I'm sorry, Heledd. I should have shown more restraint. You were right to chastise me so.'

'They will be here soon. The chamber is ready and Ceri has all her unguents and potions ready. Drink some more soup; you will need your strength.' She sipped obediently from her cup, the steam rising and dispersing in the chill of the room. Then, quite suddenly, she dropped her hands to her lap, her cup still brimming.

'Oh, God, I hope his hurt is slight.'

'The messenger said he suffered a spear thrust to the upper arm. It will not be fatal. Cadafael has had worse and lived. Our men are strong. It would take more than a poke with a stick to push either of them from this earth. It's important that you don't let him see how bad it is … even if it is the very worst it could be.'

With a whimper of distress she got up and began to pace the chamber floor.

'Oh God, let them come now.'

And at her words there came a blast of the horn at the gate and a few minutes later the first of the men came trooping into the precinct. We waited, frantically searching the weary, road-stained, faces for those we loved. There were few seriously injured, mostly walking wounded who were led away by their wives or mothers for bandaging and cosseting. Then Cadafael's horse appeared, his rich apparel mired and broken. My heart missed a beat for there was little to distinguish him as king. I darted forward, took hold of his stirrup.

'Cadafael!' I blinked the rain from my eyes, my mouth a gape of delight that he was home and safe. He slid from his saddle and I was in his arms, or he was in mine, his head drooping onto my shoulders, his beard rough on my neck. After a few moments I pulled away. 'The battle is lost?'

He shook his head, his hair stringy with sweat.

'Nay, we won it and drove them back over the Taff but at what cost I don't yet know.' He scanned the dismounting troop, his eyes dull. 'We have lost many men and many were injured, my brother among them.'

'Where is he?' My eye darted about the crowd until I spotted Ffreur's russet tunic bending over a makeshift litter. I glimpsed Iestyn's white, unmoving face, mud-spattered hair and moved forward but Cadafael held me back.

'Let her see to him. I have need of you myself.' I looked down and for the first time noticed his thick boot had been ripped open and copious gore was congealing on his shin. The blood seemed to flood from my head but somehow I gathered my wits and did not allow myself the luxury of fainting.

'Yea gods, are you hurt?' I knelt before him, trying to see the extent of the wound but he tugged at my hair.

'Inside, Heledd, help me inside, out of this infernal rain.' He leaned heavily on my shoulder as we made our way back to my bower, his step uneven, the stench of his unwashed body assaulting my nose.

'How did you do it? Is it very bad?' I pushed him into a chair, lumbered onto my knees again.

'It is nothing, just a scratch,' he protested as I drew off his boot and cut away his leggings and, when I saw that his shin was open to the bone, I swallowed down revolted fear. This was nothing? He sank backward into the chair, his head back, throat exposed, his Adam's apple standing proud. Briefly I remembered kissing it, then suddenly afraid of doing more harm than good, I struggled to my feet and ran from the room calling for Hild and Ceri.

I found them in Ffreur's chamber. Iestyn was naked on the bed, a great gash in his upper arm, his lower body covered with a great spreading purple bruise. The women worked on him with sponges while Ceri poked at the wound. I cleared my throat.

'I need some help with the King.' No one moved, they had no time for me. I spoke again. 'Hild, can you bring some water and bandages. I will tend to him myself but I will need someone to stitch his wound.'

'There is nothing to it; it's just like sewing up your sleeves.' Ceri looked up from her bloody task briefly and nodded to Hild who stopped washing the blood from Iestyn's chest and dropped her sponge into a bowl of bloody water.

Ffreur hadn't taken her eyes from Iestyn's face and I saw she clung desperately to sanity. Gwarw and Ceri bent over his torso, his chest hardly moved at all. At the foot of the bed the priest, Alric, was praying for his lord's life and Ffreur's white lips moved in unison with his. Suddenly I wished I could send a similar prayer.

Hild appeared at my side with the things I would need. 'It's simple really,' she said, 'pinch the flesh together and stitch, like you are sewing a garment.'

I backed away, a stone of sickness in my stomach. Fear for Cadafael, for myself and for my sister whom I knew would soon be widowed. Guilt stabbed at me, and not for the first time. Maybe I should have let her continue in her barren state, losing a husband was bad enough but it would be doubly hard for her without a father for her child.

Back in my chamber Cadafael had fallen asleep. At first I thought he had passed out or died but when I poked him, his gentle snores reassured me. He was exhausted, weeks of neglect and adversity, followed by debilitating injury. I took the bowl of water and ball of twine and needle from Hild and, with a jerk of my head, sent her back to Iestyn. Then I knelt at my husband's feet and wondered what to do. At the first touch of the sponge he leapt awake, his hands flying to his leg.

'Christ and all his saints, Heledd, would you kill me?'

I was stung by his words. I had been as gentle as I could and, after two more attempts to cleanse the wound, I realised he would make a poor patient. By repute he was an ogre on the battlefield but, it seemed, the ogre was made a mouse by the threat of a little pin prick. I sat back on my heels. 'Cadafael, I must wash away the gore if I am to stitch it.'

His face was a grimace of horror. 'Stitch it? You will not, woman. You have the nursing skills of a bear. Fetch Angharad and let her do it.'

My chin jutted forward. 'Angharad?' I waited for him to retract his words, his question hanging in the air between us. It was no time for jealousy but I couldn't help it. I didn't want her anywhere near him. I was his wife and I wanted to be the one to help.

'Yes, Angharad. She has some skill with wounds. Send someone to fetch her.'

I stood up, smoothed down my skirts, my jealousy almost obliterating my love. 'I will fetch her myself although, like the other servants, she is probably busy with your brother.'

It was a remark meant to chastise him but it went unnoticed so I turned on my heel and went in search of his whore. I was wrong; she wasn't with Ffreur and her husband. Instead I found her in the cooking hall, loading a tray of food for the returning King. I jerked my head to signal that she was to follow me and despite my bulk, I strode ahead of her on the way back to my bower. She followed, skimming the ground on silent feet, her movements unhindered by the trials of late pregnancy as mine were.

In the bower, she bowed to her King as if there had never been anything between them and then she knelt at his side. He did not wince as she took up the sponge and began to gently wash away the gore. With a long finger she smeared the wound with Ceri's potion, sitting back on her heels while the herbs took effect. Cadafael leaned back in his chair, his brow furrowed. I hated to see her thin brown hands on his skin, resented her proximity to him and could not erase the picture of them both knotted together in ecstasy. But I would not give her the pleasure of leaving them alone, so I watched and suffered as keenly as my husband.

I watched her prick the skin about the wound with her needle to ascertain it was numb. Then she pinched the jagged edges together as best she could and deftly stitched the two sides together. Cadafael held his breath, his tongue caught between his teeth and when it was over, he let out a great sigh of relief and smiled at her, twisting the knife deeper into my gut. Angharad leaned over him to pick up a bandage I had left on the table, her braids swinging, her breasts too close to his face. I stood up.

'You can go.' I said, without thanking her. 'I will do the rest.'

I held out my hand for the bandage and with lowered eyes she passed it to me. Then she bowed to Cadafael and silently waited for his dismissal.

'Thank you,' he said, briefly brushing her hand and she left the room with her head high, the sway of her hips and the tilt of her head exaggerated for his benefit and I wanted to kill her.

Without speaking, I knelt in her place and began to bind the wound as gently as I could before tying it in place and looking up at him. He was watching me, the beginnings of a smile flirting at the edge of his mouth.

'That's better, thank you.'

I tossed my head, still too angry to forgive him. I stood up, collected the things together. 'I will go and see how Iestyn is.' Although I wanted stay, pride prevented me and I left the room without looking back and hurried to Ffreur's chamber.

It was quieter now. His wound tidied away beneath bandages, the covers drawn up to his chin. Iestyn lay, unmoving beneath the sheet while Ffreur knelt at his bedside, her head buried in prayer. I crept to her side, touched her shoulder and she turned her head up to me.

'How is he?' I whispered, reluctant to disturb him and Ffreur got up and drew me away from the bed to the fireside.

'Oh, Heledd, I don't know, not for sure. Ceri said he will do well enough and we are praying constantly. She gave him something to make him sleep. Once he wakes, I will feel better. How is Cadafael?'

'He is sleeping too. He took a fall from his horse and opened his shin to the knee. It is nothing too serious although he is making a meal of it as men do. He is stitched and bound now and seems to be in good spirits.'

Ffreur turned back to the bed to look upon Iestyn's unmoving form. I put a hand on her shoulder. 'Ffreur, I – I will add my prayers to yours, If you think it will help, but I am certain he will recover now he is in good hands.'

In a few weeks Cadafael was hobbling about the llys but Iestyn's recovery was fraught with setbacks. First he took a long time to wake and for several days kept slipping back into unconsciousness. Ffreur was sure he would die, believing that her God would take him in exchange for allowing her a child. I did my best to comfort her but as usual I grew impatient when she refused to see things my way. It was a long and terrible month until he was able to rise from his bed and sit at the fireside but, in many ways, their weeks of convalescence was a good time for all of us. Forced as they were to spend time at the hearth, we were able to bond as a family and seek enjoyment from domestic pleasures.

Cadafael's bedtime antics were hindered a little but I did not mind, he was home and safe and for a little while I was freed from worrying about the wars. Ffreur and Iestyn, who were as much in love as ever, made the most of the time together and Ffreur bustled about him like a good wife.

Even the summer decided at last to put an end to winter and May blossomed into sunshine. I began to look forward to my confinement, the ever-increasing girth of my belly making me long for my usual agility and a return to love making.

'It's a shame you are too large for loving, Heledd. All this inactivity increases a man's ardour.'

I glared at him from my chair. 'Does it, indeed, my lord? My heart bleeds for you.'

He let out a bark of laughter at my taciturnity and I scowled at him again. 'You can have no idea how it feels to be like a great whale, unable to enjoy even the simplest of human pleasures and I would prefer it if you didn't rub my shortcomings in my face.'

He laughed again, groped for his stick and got up to stump across the chamber to me. Planting a kiss on my head, he limped to the door.

'I will leave you awhile, Wife. Give you time to rediscover your temper. A turn about the precinct will cool my blood too.'

When he was gone I threw down my distaff. 'Curses be upon him!' I sank into a dark mood, following him in my mind as he took his turn about the llys. I was certain he had gone to Angharad and that the little strumpet would be glad to cool his ardour. Misery crashed into my chest like a lance and, dashing away a tear, I yelled for Gwarw to help me to the refuge of my bed.

Many hours later I opened my eyes, wondering what had woken me. The chamber was in darkness, only the glow of the night brazier illuminating the outline of the bed.

Cadafael was absent but, from the gentle tic of Hild's breathing on her truckle bed and the rumbling snores of Gwarw in her closet, I knew I was not alone. I pulled myself onto my pillow and reached for my night-time cup and, as I did so, I felt a gentle pop and warm liquid gushed onto the mattress. The child was coming ... at last.

I waited for a while to be sure and once the pains were becoming regular, I called out for Hild. She sat up, rubbing her eyes, her tunic crumpled, her hair scat up the back of her head. Struggling to her feet, she fumbled through the dark to the bed.

'Lady?'

'The child is coming, Hild. Can you wake Gwarw and then run to fetch Ceri?'

A few minutes more and the chamber was alive with activity. Hild threw on her cloak and slipped from the door and Gwarw began to stoke the fires, refuel the brazier and set water to boil. I lay on my pillow, untroubled by the toil to come.

I had done it before and could do again. 'I hope you are a girl.' I whispered to the taut lump of my belly, enjoying the vision of a small fair girl child, with wide blue eyes. A new happy time was ahead. I was sure I would have a girl and once Ffreur had birthed her son, my joy would be shared, and shared joy is the gladdest joy of all.

I was right not to worry. The birth was straightforward and two hours later I was sitting up in bed with my daughter in my arms. I cannot say how glad she made me, I beamed upon the company and felt quite sure I would never utter a cross word again.

Ffreur burst into the chamber wrapping a shawl about her nightgown.

'Why didn't anyone call me?' She leaned over the bed, peeled back the blanket, tears springing from her eyes. 'Oh, Heledd, she is beautiful.'

I let her take the child from me and she sat back, cradling the bundle to her chest, dipping her face to smell her hair. 'Does she have a name?'

I had been waiting for that question. 'Oh, I think we shall call her Ffreur.' I could not prevent the smugness from spreading across my face as I watched her absorb my answer.

Sometimes it is not easy to find and hold real happiness but that quiet moment with my sister and my newborn daughter was so perfect that it has stayed with me forever. When I think of my Ffreurs, it is as they were then, my sister replete with child and pink with delight, with her namesake cradled in her arms.

Eight

'Come along, Ceri.' She was infuriatingly slow, placing small bottles deep within her basket, folding lints and bandages to lie beside them. 'We cannot wait, hurry.' I grabbed her hand and dragged her from the hovel, leaving the door still swinging on its hinges as we struggled up the hill toward the llys. My shift tangled about my feet, tripping me, hindering me when every one of my instincts urged me to make haste.

So quickly did I drive her that her breath gusted forth in great gasps and, when we came to a steeper incline and she began to fail, I placed a hand on each of her vast buttocks and propelled her forward.

'More haste, less speed,' she chastised but I ignored her and hurried her onward. Then, as we passed beneath the gate, a scream rent the air from the direction of the ladies bower and Ceri's movements at last became more urgent. We burst through the door and Ceri, at last realising my urgency, dropped her basket and hurried to the bed. I leaned over my sister and put a hand to her burning forehead.

'It is alright, Ffreur. I was as quick as I could be.'

'Heledd,' she clung to me. Her hair was plastered to her head, her legs bedaubed in blood.

I turned to Ceri. 'You must help her. I will give you all I possess, anything. Just help her.'

The panic in my own voice unnerved me. Ceri, her face grey and serious, came slowly toward the bed, putting a hand on my sister's stomach, another to her groin.

'The child is lying wrong.' Her voice was muted, her face unreadable.

'You can help her though, can't you?' I watched her go to the fire for warm water and begin to wash the blood from Ffreur's legs.

'I don't know.'

This was not the woman I knew, the woman who had dragged me and my child from death, taken away my pain, healed my petty sicknesses. This was not the powerful being that had touched mine and Ffreur's souls in the moonlight.

I gave a short humourless laugh. 'Of course you can.'

Her eyes did not meet mine, her mouth worked for a while, the whiskers on her chin, glinting. 'I can only try, the child is askew. I can try to straighten it and if the gods will it, she will live. If they don't, then there is nothing I can do.'

I sat back on my heels, uncomprehending of her words and, for a few fleeting seconds, imagined life without Ffreur, an idea so unbearable that I thrust it quickly away. I would rather die myself.

I stood up and Ffreur groaned, groped for my hand. I leaned over her. 'I am not leaving, I will be back.'

Dragging Ceri by the shawl, I thrust her against the wall, looked deep into her eyes. 'You must save her, Ceri, there is no other alternative. I believe in you, I know you can do it and I have gold, treasures. I will reward you well. I will make you rich.'

She nodded uncertainly and moved away. On her way to the bed she whispered something to Hild who slipped from the room. I dabbed my sister's forehead with a damp rag.

'Oh, Heledd,' she whispered. 'It hurts so much. However did you bear it?'

My throat closed and I struggled to find my voice. 'We are fashioned to bear it, Ffreur. Be at peace, all will be well.'

I thought of my new-born daughter lying cosy in her cradle, and of her brothers tumbled like puppies in their bed. I recalled the ease with which I had borne them. I had carried them high and delivered them promptly. Why was it not like that for Ffreur?

Ceri leaned over the bed, her face close to my sister's. 'I am going to try to shift the child. It will hurt so I want you to drink this for the pain.'

She struggled to sit up. I supported her, held the cup to her lips, felt the feverish heat from her body. And after a while, as I stoked her hand, she slipped into sleep and Ceri lifted her dormant knees and spread her legs wide.

Ffreur jumped at the first touch and when Ceri reached in to locate the baby's head, her eyes flew open. She opened her mouth, emitting an unworldly noise the like of which I had never heard outside the farmyard. I hoped Cadafael kept Iestyn far from the bower and safely out of earshot.

My tears fell, on our hands, on her face and I could not stop them. It was worse than death to sit by and witness her torture, to try to quiet her writhing body, to still her flaying arms. If I could have, I would have absorbed all of her pain.

Ceri worked for an hour, massaging the distorted bulge of Ffreur's belly, forcing the baby to turn, hurting her, making her scream. There was blood on my lips where I had bitten them and my hands shook as if I had ague. Every so often Ffreur slipped from consciousness, lying prone upon the scarlet sheets, her limbs contorted until the pain returned to drag her horribly back to reality.

'The child is straighter but I fear the after birth is blocking the birth canal, we must see how she goes.' Ceri stood up and wiped her brow, leaving a streak of scarlet. 'It is up to her now but I don't know if she has the strength.'

We gave her an infusion of herbs to rouse her, fortify her.

I leaned over her. 'You must push now, my love, and your babe will be here soon.'

'If he lives,' Ceri murmured, and I shot her a killing glance.

Ffreur strained and pushed for a further hour or more but the child did not budge. In between spasms she begged me to look after Iestyn and her babe, should it live and her features were so marred with agony that she no longer bore any resemblance to my pretty sister.

Sweat glistened on her face, her eyes were hollow. 'Heledd,' she croaked at last. 'Send for the priest.'

I did not want to. To send for a priest was to admit defeat, but, for Ffreur's easement, I nodded to Ceri to send a messenger. Then I gave a tight little smile and tried to make my voice light.

'You always make so much fuss, Ffreur. You will not die, for God loves you too well.'

Her clammy hand rested on my arm, a claw of a hand, daubed with blood and mucus. 'I am not afraid to die, Heledd. Although I have sinned, God will forgive me and all will be well.'

I bit down upon a sob, tossed back my hair, my voice issuing harsher than I intended. 'You have not sinned, Ffreur, and you will live. Your child will live and thrive and we will all be happy. You and I, Cadafael and Iestyn, together with our children. Just as we planned.'

She did not believe me but her eyes were calm. 'Look after my baby, Heledd. Raise him to be strong, like you. Promise me.'

My eyes were blind. My will screamed against the gods, all of them. They would not do this to me. They would not have Ffreur. I would dance with the very devil to stop it.

Wrenching open the door, I yelled for Hild who arrived, panting, a short time later. I told her to fetch me a knife from the kitchens and Ceri stood up slowly, reading my mind, foreseeing my plan.

Shaking her head, she began to back away. 'I cannot,' she said, her hands atremble and I saw then that she was afraid.

Ffreur whimpered, her voice increasing until she growled and screamed like an animal. I held her, my tears spouting afresh.

'I am here, Ffreur. Just keep breathing. Remember the song we sang at my childbed.' I began to hum, desperately trying to recall the chant we had used. 'Ceri, come here, now.' I yelled at her, losing control, dragging her to the floor beside me. 'Fix it, Ceri. Fix it, like you always do.'

My body shook. I was on the brink of insanity when suddenly Hild appeared, a beastly looking blade in her hand. Her eyes were wild, her mouth squared at the unfolding horror. Ffreur had passed out again, given a few moments release.

I grabbed Hild's arm. 'Where were you?'

'I was in the chapel,' she replied, 'Ceri told me to pray, and so I did. '

I think that is the moment that I finally knew we were lost.

There was not much time, Ffreur's lapse of consciousness lasting only moments. I backed Ceri into a corner. 'You must do it. Cut the child from her. There is no other choice.'

She shook her head mutely. 'I cannot, they would curse me as a witch should she die.'

Ffreur stirred on the bed, another assault imminent. She could not last much longer. Her strength was failing and the relief between contractions was growing so short it was giving her no respite. She must either give birth now, or die. At that moment I hated Ceri and, poking her hard on the shoulder, I spoke through gritted teeth.

'Instruct me then.'

Ceri and Hild held torches aloft over the bed, the light flickered and sweat dripped onto my hands. Hild whimpered, the farmyard odour of her fright pervading the room but Ceri was calm, her face tense and watchful. Ffreur lay, half dead on the bed, her grotesque belly taut, her thighs smeared with scarlet. With each fresh pain she strained afresh but imperceptibly, the potion Ceri had brewed worked its way to her brain. Her limbs became less agitated and her breathing slowed. Soon, it was impossible to tell if her breast rose and fell at all.

Ceri swore that the afterbirth was blocking the path that the babe was supposed to take, that was why there was so much blood. There was no other way. I had heard of children being cut alive from the womb but had no idea of how to go about it. I knew no one who had survived it but I steeled myself and looked at the girl on the bed.

This was my sister, whom I had loved since I was two years old and my mother had first let me peek into her basket. I would not let her die.

With a sopping rag I washed the blood from her belly. Ceri leaned over my shoulder. 'It's best to go in low, where the babe's head should be, I think.' I hoped I did not slit its throat. Ffreur would never forgive me.

I pressed the knife tip against her belly, made a slight indentation, my hand shaking. Then I hesitated, looked up at Ffreur's stringy, wet hair, her alabaster face beaded with sweat and knew I had no choice, I must act now or lose her.

I had thought her flesh would slice like pork but I had to push down as hard as I could to cut through the skin and tissue. Ffreur barely stirred and I prayed I was not too late, maybe the potion had been lethal. I glanced up to Ceri and Hild who, with their breath suspended in their throats, watched my every move.

Blood spurted, marring my view, and I signalled for Ceri to pour water to cleanse the yawning wound and saw, through the film of Ffreur's womb, the curled limbs of a child.

Hild grizzled aloud, a drip of snot hanging from her nose, her face glazed with sweat, the torch waving erratically. I took a breath, looked from one to the other. Ceri moved her mouth in silent encouragement and, feeling her camaraderie, I drew my knife firmly across the membrane. It split asunder, like silk.

A gush of water and the sweet, familiar smell of birth fluid. I delved into my sister's womb and grasped the pulsing body of her child. It was hot, slippery, and I struggled for a firm grip. Knotting my fingers about its ankles, I ripped the child from its mother and severed the cord.

Without so much as glancing at it, I thrust the baby into Hild's waiting arms and she began to rub it briskly with the hem of her apron. She still bawled like an infant but the child made no noise at all. I turned back to the bed.

Ffreur was a mess. Her body mutilated by my knife. The sheets smothered in gore. Panic threatened to engulf me again. I could feel it rising and knew it would soon overspill.

I turned to Ceri, my eyes wild, my throat knotted, my chin wobbling. 'What now?' She stumbled forward. 'You have to sew her up, like a battle wound.'

'What with?'

I wanted it all to end. My body longed to collapse, my mind craved oblivion. Ceri rummaged in her bag, brought forth some twine but then, seeing my face, she hesitated, let out a breath.

'Go and sit at her head, child. I will do it.'

My legs shook, my hands trembled like an age-bitten woman's. Gratefully, I stumbled to the stool. Unable to believe what I had done, I took a deep breath, filling my lungs with fresher air and blew out again hard, seeking to calm my raging blood.

I sat at Ffreur's head, held her hand, talked to her, sang her favourite songs, my voice catching and tremulous. Her breath was so slight that even when I held my hand in front of her mouth I could not feel it. In the opposite corner Hild fussed over the child. It had barely made a sound and I did not care. I had not asked if it were a boy or girl.

I clung to my Ffreur, watching for her breathing to grow stronger, for her colour to return, longing for her eyes to flicker open, dying for her smile but, although I sat there until morning, her eyes never opened and that smile never came.

PART FIVE
LAMENT FOR PENGWERN

The Hall of Cyndylan is dark
To-night, without fire, without candle!

655 AD

On the day we lay Ffreur beneath the earthen floor of the llys chapel, I thought I had reached the bottommost depth of grief. Although it was summer, a steady drenching drizzle fell, blanketing our spirits further. Poor Iestyn, his head lowered in the scudding rain, wept as we trailed back to the llys but I could not comfort him.

I threw off the old gods who had forsaken me, ignored my most fervent prayers, and now I sought the comfort of the ancient priest that had been Ffreur's confessor. I unburdened my soul to him, confessed my darkest deeds but his ears were so gummed up with other people's sin that he could not hear my words.

I needed to be scourged, whipped without mercy but he did not even castigate me verbally. All he did was wipe his own sorry tears and offer me shrift before sending me back to my children and the comforts of my nurse. I knew that I was not yet forgiven. I had meddled with God's will and, should my death come unexpectedly, I would burn in the flames of hell.

My two-month-old daughter, Ffreur, was dark haired with piercing black eyes, and as unlike my sister as could be, but she gave me some small comfort. We named Ffreur's son Ianto but I could not bear to look upon him. Although he was small and sickly, his spine twisted and probably his mind too, he clung stubbornly to life. I reluctantly allowed him into my nursery but whenever I looked at him, God forgive me, I wished that he had died instead of his mother.

Those early days are hard to think on. Ffreur's death plunged us all into gloom. Everyone had loved her, for her sunny nature had brightened even the cloudiest day and, forgetting my part in her downfall, I hated Iestyn for wanting a child so much that she risked her life to give him one. And he, in turn, blamed me for my intervention.

In the first hours of his grief he raged at me. 'You should never have used the knife; you have killed her with your incompetence.'

The sting of those words lacerate me yet and in the weeks that followed I grew thin, neither eating nor sleeping and, when my milk dried and Gwarw arranged a wet nurse for baby Ffreur, I grieved afresh at having to pass her into the care of another woman.

But, in the night, when I leapt screaming from sleep, fresh from a dream in which my knife still dripped with my sister's blood, Cadafael held me tight and I clung to him like a drowning woman to a rock.

Two

It was a subdued party that left the llys to attend Cynddylan's wedding. We took horse to the coast where the royal ships of Gwynedd bobbed at their mooring. The sting of the salt wind bit some colour into my cheeks and my heart twisted painfully as I realised how much Ffreur would have loved to have been there. I imagined her clinging to the ships rail, the wind shredding her pretty hair and when Gwarw asked me why I wept, I blamed my streaming eyes upon the lively wind.

The sky was like a bright blanket of lapis lazuli stretched high above us where gulls turned and dived, their regretful cries like the syllables of a lament. Cadafael and I stood at the prow, the spume in our faces, the wind tugging at our cloaks and penetrating the lacings and folds of our clothing. I rested my head on his shoulder, frail and exhausted after weeks of misery.

'It will be good to visit your childhood home again, will it not?'

I looked at his profile that stood out sharply against the backdrop of the sky. The sea breeze blew his hair from his face, accentuating the square line of his jaw, the sensuous curve of his mouth. In a flood of gratitude that I still had him, I sent up a little prayer of thanks.

'There will be memories,' I said, unwilling to mention Ffreur's name. His chest rose and fell and when he lowered his eyes to mine I noticed the shadows of strain about his eyes and mouth and realised for the first time that it had been hard for him too. I cursed myself for a selfish, thoughtless woman. I would do better in the future and try to be as thoughtful a wife as my sister had been.

'Memories are everywhere, my love, but one day, God willing, they will cease to be painful and you will remember only happy times.'

I tucked my head onto his shoulder again, feeling safe. There was no other place I wanted to be. 'There were lots of happy times,' I whispered and he held me, without speaking, pretending not to see the drops that fell upon my breast.

Three

At less than fourteen summers Cynddylan's affianced bride, Rhonwen was like a puppy, full of childlike warmth. Although she tried to adopt a funereal expression she failed miserably and greeted me instead lovingly, her dark eyes dancing, her step light with her own joy. She had a similar sunny nature to Ffreur and although I was just twenty-four she made me feel like an old woman.

Because of Ffreur's death her marriage celebrations would be muted but she allowed no resentment to show and, knowing I would come to genuinely love her, I forced myself to smile and express delight at Cynddylan's choice. And when he came tripping down the hall steps, darkly handsome in his purple cloak, he embraced me before them all, his grief for our sister vibrating from deep within, so that only I knew of it.

He pulled away, looked down at me. 'Thank God I still have you, Heledd.'

He hugged me again and at his shared sorrow, a sob broke free from my throat. Although we had many siblings, Cynddylan, Cynwraith, Ffreur and I shared the same mother and that drew us closer, our misery somehow intensified by shared blood.

But life goes on and those about us began to shake off sorrow to enjoy the celebration. Cadafael's household teulu mingled with Cynddylan's whose hospitality was famous and that night, while the harp was passed from hand to hand and the leaping flames reflected in the metalwork of the swinging lanterns and set the warrior's gold gleaming, I sat in my old place at the high table and looked with sadness about the familiar hall.

Beside me, where Ffreur should have been, was Rhonwen, full of enthusiasm for her new life, and while my throat ached for by-gone days, when our hearts had borne so much hope, she looked forward to a life of love and children. Too despondent to eat properly, I picked at the food that Rhonwen heaped upon my platter and I only pretended to drink. I was tired, from both grief and the exertion of the journey and I longed to retire to the chamber I would share with Cadafael. My bed called to me. I craved to be there with him, closeted away from the world, which was so cruel.

Gwarw and Hild were elsewhere, tucking the children into strange beds, comforting their fears whilst here in the hall Angharad, her upright frame clothed in one of my discarded yellow tunics, wove in and out the company, refilling cups, the object of male appreciation.

I watched her dully, no longer caring that she was fairer than I, and as I watched she leaned over Cadafael's chair, filling not just his cup but his eye, silently challenging him to reach for her as he has so often done. I narrowed my eyes and saw his lips move, the smile he gave her stabbing me like a knife.

I did not know if he still visited her and did not dare to enquire but I hated her. My heart full of jealous resentment I decided to make a bridal gift of her to Rhonwen before we left and be rid of her for good.

I had made so many mistakes, so many wanton actions that could not now be undone and I suffered so many regrets. Rhonwen, noticing my despondency, nudged my elbow and lifted her cup, encouraging me to do the same.

'Drink up, Heledd. The musicians will be here soon,' she said. 'We have some fine entertainers … but you know that, of course. I was forgetting this is your home.'

I stirred myself, unwilling to darken her mood and conjured up a smile.

'Yes,' I replied. 'In my father's day the entertainment was said to be the best in Powys, people came from far and wide.'

It was true, my father had loved the revels, and minstrels had travelled long distances to sing in our famous hall. In those days, of course, we were at peace and the land made for safer travelling. Now, the war with Oswiu made the very air bitter and the women complained that talk of conflict tainted every feast.

Even now I could hear Cynddylan and Cadafael debating when to strike next against the North Umbrian King and my heart fluttered at the idea of him leaving so soon. All men, even my strong, handsome husband, were vulnerable in war. If it wasn't a blade that killed them, it could be the fever or execution if they were captured.

The last assault on North Umbria had been victorious, with Oswald made so nervous that he had offered an alliance between his son and Penda's eldest daughter. Luckily for her, King Penda refused, renewing his hostilities against the north until he held the army under siege at Bebbanburg.

King Penda's realm expanded all the time, his ring of allies forming a strong band against the greedy Oswiu. He would not rest until the North Umbrians were entirely crushed. We expected Penda's arrival any day now, and to the women's chagrin the men's fighting blood was roused and the wedding plans quickly deteriorated into a war council.

I had not the stomach for war and the voices of Cadafael and Cynwraith, together with those of Cyndyylan and my cousin, Urien, wearied me. Life was too short to be spent in bloodletting. I turned my attention to the musicians.

A ring of fire-lit faces, the sound of the harp, the crackle of flames took me back to the last night of my girlhood. The night I had first seen Osian and afterwards lay with him beneath an autumn moon. I wondered if he would sing tonight and if he had altered in any way. So, when he stepped into the ring of firelight, I was not surprised to see he had not changed at all.

The strong bones of his face gleamed in the leaping light of the torches, his hair and beard shining red in the way that had delighted me of old. His song was of a sailor, lost upon the seas, the rich tones of his voice soaring to the blackened rafters but although he looked and sang just the same, my heart did not falter and neither did my pulse quicken.

I watched him, noted the circle of entranced young girls at his feet and realised that I was the one who had changed. I had grown up while he had not. Osian was all he would ever be while I had fledged into womanhood and, to my relief, his dilute charms no longer touched me. I had been afraid that once I saw him things between us would be as they had ever been but it was not so. I turned my eyes away from the pretty picture he made.

Further along the table Cadafael argued affably with my brothers, jabbing a finger on the map he had sketched with his dagger on the board. I was as physically aware of his presence as if he were physically touching me. I sensed rather than saw Cadafael. I did not need to look at him to know when he thrust a hand through his dark hair or whether he smiled or frowned. We were now so complete a couple that we seemed to breathe from one set of lungs.

I observed him now. His brow was furrowed with some argument he presented to Cynddylan, and as I watched him and Osian's song went on and on in the background, I came to realise that I was fickle in love, for it was my husband who moved me now. He was no longer a substitute for a lost love. Cadafael was the real thing.

The last note of the harp reverberated about the hall and Osian bowed, his leg long and elegant, and when he straightened up, shaking back his hair from his face, he looked directly at me, his smile all it had ever been. I realised then, as our eyes met across the smoke-filled hall that his love for me remained unchanged and that tonight he would look for me in the shadow of the yew trees.

Four

Word came that Oswiu had left his North Umbrian holding and was marching on Pengwern. Poor Rhonwen's wedding plans were laid aside and the talk was now only of war. The marriage would have to wait. My brother, Elfan, rode in from his Kingdom on the northern reaches of Powys and I stood in the dust and waited for his greeting. It was long since I had seen him.

'Can this be Heledd?' He pulled me close for a kiss and I tried not to wrinkle my nose for he was rank with the stench of travelling. 'Our scouts spotted Penda and his armies on the road, they are but two days ride away.'

Elfan kept his arm about my shoulder as Cynddylan gripped his hand and slapped him on the back. 'It's good to see you, little brother. We are all assembled. Morfaed, Cynon and Gwion with their hearth troop, even our uncles are come, although they are too old to bear the sword. Together with Gwynedd and Penda's men, this time we will smash Oswiu, once and for all.'

'It has been a long time coming,' grinned Elfan.

The two men moved toward the assembled warriors who were cleaning and honing their weapons. Braziers burned in the yard where servants sweated as they burnished the armour and horse trappings to a rich, glow. A chill wind sprang across the settlement and I pulled my cloak close about me as I made my way back to the women's bower and ducked beneath the lintel.

'Heledd.' Rhonwen rose and linked my arm as Ffreur would have done and I guessed she had taken instruction from Cynddylan to look to my comfort. I warmed toward her even more. 'We are all busy sewing colours for our men to carry into battle. Would you come and help me sort the threads? What are Cadafael's colours?'

We knelt on the fireside furs and began to arrange the silks into different shades but I had little enthusiasm for the task. My heart wasn't in it and from time to time I paused to look about me. Set aside from the others, Angharad worked her spindle, a pile of yarn growing at her feet. My eye did not linger with her but wandered restlessly about the room.

The walls were lined with springtime tapestries, bright floral colours befitting a women's bower, and the central hearth was bright, the cinders swept and the floor rushes sprinkled with aromatic fennel and lavender. Close to the hearth Gwarw and Hild kept my children amused with counting and clapping games. I put aside the silks and went to join them.

As I passed I noticed Baby Ffreur stirring in her basket and I picked her up, delighted when her milky mouth opened in greeting. It was impossible not to smile in reply. I propped her against my shoulder, rubbing her back, smelling her hair. Her little head bobbed as, fixing her eye upon my gold and amber shoulder clasps, she struggled to hold it firm. Moments like this, when I was filled with maternal love for my children were the closest I ever came to contentment. I sniffed her cold, damp cheek and stroked the fragile scalp feeling the life pulse beneath.

'She is feeding well?'

The wet nurse stood up and bobbed a greeting. 'Oh, yes, Lady, like a piglet and she grows day by day.'

I began to pace the chamber, humming a nursery tune beneath my breath. All my children had gained weight rapidly in their early months and I thanked my newfound God that they had all thrived. When they grew to manhood my sons would help forge a stronger alliance between my husband and brothers and, when my daughter grew, she would marry well to increase her father's power and influence.

But it was not the same for Ianto. He was sickly and a finicky feeder, taking just a few drops before falling asleep, only to wake twenty minutes later and puke it all up again. His nurse despaired of him and we all wondered how long he would survive. I walked to where he lay, swathed in blankets in the depths of his cot and felt a twist of resentment that he lived and my sister had died. The cruel irony of my healthy, pious sister perishing to give life to a sickly, twisted monster ripped at my heart.

I took some comfort from the fact that Ianto would probably not survive his first year. His face bore a slight tinge of blue and veins were traced upon his bald scalp, the skin stretched tight across his skull like face. He was like a tiny effigy of death. I shuddered and turned away. Even Iestyn could barely look at him, blaming the child for his mother's death, wishing he had never been born ... as we all did.

Five

My brothers and I were in the compound when Penda's cavalcade arrived. He slid from his mount, his personality immediately engulfing us all. With his usual affability he embraced Cynddylan, clapped Cadafael on the back and slung an arm about Cynwraith's neck. Then he saw me and fixed me with his eye, opened his mouth in a gaping smile, making me flush and lower my head in embarrassment.

'Lady,' he cried. 'Don't stand on ceremony with me.' He flung his arms around me, swamping me with the stink of his bearskin cloak and, before I managed to disentangle myself, he somehow managed to furtively squeeze my right breast. I smoothed my tunic, steadied my breathing and glanced at Cadafael, who raised an ironic eyebrow at my discomfiture. I grimaced at him and, smothering a laugh, he came up beside me to clasp my hand and, thus protected, I followed the company across the enclosure and into the main hall.

It took a while to accustom our eyes to the gloom but neither Penda's pace nor voice faltered as he outlined his plans. I heard Cynddylan agreeing with him, Cynwraith advising on which the path the outriders should take, and as the shadowy outlines of the those present grew sharper as my eyes adjusted to the dark, I realised I was the only woman present in a company of men. My elderly but well-respected uncles were nodding sagely, listening to the strategies of the younger men and offering advice where it was needed. Their bodies might be too weak to fight but their minds were as sharp as knives.

Cynddylan put his foot on a stool and leaned over Penda's shoulder to consult the parchment map. He nodded slowly, indicated the best places to ford the River Trent. Cadafael was beside me, our legs touching, his fingers wrapped in the fabric of my tunic. He leaned closer, his breath whispering on my cheek. 'I must involve myself in this, my love, for we ride out at dawn, but you and I have some business before that.'

My belly turned a small lusty somersault and I squeezed his hand. 'I will wait for you.' Before I quit the hall, his lips lingered on my inner wrist where the blood raced just below the surface of my skin. When I reached the door, I turned in time to catch his lop-sided smile as he winked an eye in farewell.

Six

'My eyes are sore.' Hedyn rubbed his grubby fingers into his eye sockets and moaned. He had been complaining for a few days now, and I knew from my own childhood the misery of sore eyes in a smoke filled room.

Feeling in need of air myself, I put down my needlework. 'What you need is some teasel water. Shall we go for a walk to gather some?'

Hedyn brightened up instantly, glad to be released from the confines of my bower. My mother used to bathe my own sore eyes with water collected from the leaves of the teasel and I knew it would offer him easement. We crossed the enclosure hand in hand. It was not often Hedyn and I were alone, usually my eldest son dominated the scene but today was different and Hedyn made the most of it, directing the conversation and relishing the attention.

It was a still day, the sky blanketed with white cloud, the birds silent. The only sound was the rustling of the wind in the tall grasses but as we began to cross the boggy field, tiptoeing to find a dry path, a flock of starlings flew up, their black bodies peppering the sky. We tilted back our heads and watched them for a while.

'Look at them all,' Hedyn cried. 'There must be thousands.'

We raised a hand to our brows to see them loop and twist in a black ribbon toward the horizon.

'Too many to count,' I agreed and, taking his hand again, we made to go on our way but a voice suddenly breaking the silence behind me, made my heart almost leap from my body.

'Just think of the size of the pie that many birds would fill.'

Hedyn and I spun around. I put a hand to my chest, knowing before I turned who I would find. After a brief glance at my face, Osian squatted down in front of Hedyn. It was apparent from his tender manner that he had recognised his own son. His voice, when it came was a little hoarse, as if he had been weeping. 'Good morrow,' he said, gently. 'What is your name?'

Delighted to have doubled his adult audience in an instant, Hedyn beamed upon him. 'I am Prince Hedyn,' he made a short bow, 'and this is my mother, Queen Heledd.'

Osian stood up. His blue eyes were keen, his Adam's apple working in his throat, betraying his emotion. With a jolt of shame I remembered kissing it and looked away.

'Your mother and I have met before.'

His fingers were on mine, his lips on the back of my hand. I swallowed, not knowing what to say, unable to meet his eye. 'Where are you going?' Osian ushered us along the path. 'We may as well all walk together.'

'I have sore eyes and Mother knows a cure, so we are fetching the remedy that she says grows by the river.'

Osian eyes bore deep into my face and I felt myself reddening, an increasing need to run away.

'I thought you must have been crying,' he said without looking at the child.

Hedyn looked affronted. 'I never cry. Well, not unless you count the time Cynfcddw walloped me with a bag of stone counters.'

I placed my hand on my son's ruddy head, stroked his hair, noting at first hand that it was the exact shade as his father's.

Osian was impressed. 'You are a brave lad. I wouldn't be surprised if even a seasoned warrior would have shed tears at that.' He cocked a smile at me before continuing. 'And you are a very handsome lad too, if I may say so.'

The child was a replica of himself and before I could stop it, a glimmer of mirth made my mouth twitch. I had forgotten his sense of humour. The tension lifted a little as we moved through the long grasses which, in places, reached my shoulder. While Hedyn ran ahead, leaping to try to see over the top to the river, Osian remained at my side. 'I have been trying to see you.'

At his words the panic increased again. I did not look at him. I just wanted him to bid us good day and walk away but I knew he wasn't going anywhere, not until he'd had some answers. 'I know,' I whispered, 'but it is dangerous, unwise. We risk too much.'

He grabbed my hand. 'I would risk death for you, Heledd. I have before.'

I snatched back my hand. 'That is exactly what we do risk, right now, just talking like this. If anyone should guess …'

Hedyn came running back, waving a feather. 'Look at this, Mother, it is so pretty. I shall make a gift of it to Medwyl.'

I bent over his treasure, murmuring appreciation, stroking its softness and all the time I could feel Osian's eyes upon us. When Hedyn ran off again I wanted to call him back, use him as a shield against his father's searching questions.

'So what has changed, Heledd? In the beginning it was you that sought after me. You were the one that laughed at my fears, and again, in Gwynedd, when we made this child together, you were prepared to risk everything.'

'I – I have to be careful …'

Anger and pain was beginning to colour his face, his eyes protruding slightly as he realised I was making excuses. I had made such a mess of so many people's lives. Ffreur's, Iestyn's, Ianto's, Osian's … but the memory of those heady, smoky nights at Ceri's hearth came flooding back. I had forgotten his gentleness, the sorcery of his personality and as we stood sheltered in the wavering grasses, I felt myself sway.

'I have to think of my children, especially Hedyn, who is so vulnerable. Seeing you both together … it is obvious.'

He reached up and touched my face and I flinched as if his fingers were red hot. 'No-one will see us together. I swear it.'

I felt his pull. His blue eyes swam with tears, his longing difficult to refuse. I wavered toward him and his hand touched my waist, his eyes began to merge into one ... and then I remembered Cadafael and snapped awake.

I stepped away. 'No, I am sorry. I cannot. I must think of my family.'

In truth, I didn't really want him, but as usual I was just too easily persuaded and not thinking straight. Had Cadafael been there for comparison I would not have hesitated to choose him over Osian. I needed to escape from the confrontation but as I turned away, he lunged for me. I swerved off the path, paddling through muck to avoid him, the wet striking through my shoes, but I was not quick enough. He caught my hand, held it fast and hauled me out of the mire and into his arms. His lips were hot on my neck, his hands roaming my body.

I had never been afraid of him, never realised the day would come when he would use his superior strength against me. I struggled to loosen his grip but he was too strong and his hot mouth smeared across mine.

'Mother?'

Hedyn's quiet voice severed Osian's grip. He sprang away from me, his face red, his eyes guilty, his chest heaving as we stood surveying one another, each knowing it was over between us.

Angrily, I grabbed my son's hand and dragged him back the way we had come, through the long grass, across the meadow, along the riverbank and up the hill toward the llys. He had to run fast to keep up with the furious pace I set but I did not slow my step until his laboured breath made me realise his distress.

At the gate I stopped, looked down at his scarlet face and squatted before him, careless of the hem of my tunic dangling in the dust. Tears had forged a muddy track down his cheeks, making his eyes look sorer than ever. I hugged him. 'Don't worry, Sweeting. I am alright.'

He sniffed and wiped his nose on the back of his hand. 'Why did that man do that to you? Is he a bad man? Did he want to hurt you?'

'No. No, of course not. He is an old friend. He was just very pleased to see me again, that is all.'

The boy thought for a while. 'And do you like him, Mother?'

I took a deep breath. 'He was my playmate once but now I am a grown up, I do not want his friendship any longer.'

Hedyn's brow furrowed, his face contorted as he wrestled with this information.

'Will Medwyl not want to be my friend when she becomes a woman?'

'Oh, I am sure she will. It is different with you two for you are half-siblings. Her father is your father and that makes it different. Now, I don't think we should tell anyone about what happened. I wouldn't want Osian to get into trouble. Can it be our secret?'

He nodded. 'Very well, Mother, I liked him at first. I thought he was our friend. And he had such nice crinkly eyes.'

'Yes,' I said and stood up, smoothing my skirts. As we passed beneath the outer gate Hedyn fished the feather from his pocket. It was somewhat spoiled now but he smoothed it as best he could with his fingers.

'I wish Medwyl wasn't my sister,' he said, ' then I could wed her, when I am a man.'

Angharad was just disappearing into the women's bower when we entered the gate. Hedyn, spotting his siblings, ran off happily to play and I hoped he would soon forget the incident. He was a sensitive child, far more bothered by small things than his elder brother and of the two boys, he was the one I worried about.

Cynfeddw would always cope with whatever problems life threw at him; I had no worries on that score. He was competent and selfish enough to always come out on top. Hedyn was another matter. I watched him approach Medwyl and show her the feather. She smiled her wide smile and poked it into her waistband before taking his hand and leading him off to play. Of course, they weren't siblings at all and there was no likeness between them. But for my duplicitous ways there would have been no bar to marriage between them but now that was something I must never let happen. Should their attachment grow it were better they were kept apart than my own sin be exposed. I lingered for a while, pondering the problems of family and the future until, satisfied that he was already forgetting what he had witnessed in the meadow, I went inside and gestured for a drink.

Angharad's face was unusually flushed when she brought it and I noticed she was a little out of breath. She gave a reluctant bow.

'Where have you been, Madam?' she asked, handing me the cup, and I answered without thinking.

'Hedyn and I went to the river to collect teasels.'

'But where are they, then?' She cast a glance about the chamber, her eyes gleaming darkly as if something had excited her.

'I couldn't see any within my reach. I will send a boy for them later.' She stood, clutching her tray, her eyes hiding something, and annoyed by her constant presence, I flicked her away as if she were a wasp.

Seven

I slept for a while before supper so as to be fresh when Cadafael came to me later. When I awoke, revived and freshened by sleep, I stretched my limbs and called to Gwarw to help me into my saffron tunic. She fastened it with my favourite amber clasps and then brought a stool so I could sit while she dressed my hair. She drew the comb through it, teasing out the tangles, before looping and twisting the knee length braids about my ears. I always enjoyed such ministrations and I closed my eyes, giving myself up to the gentle rhythm of her busy fingers. When she was done I stood up and held out my arms for her inspection.

'You'll do,' she said. 'Now, hurry along, the company are waiting.'

The hall was crowded, the air rich with the aroma of roasting meat, and smoke curled about the carved timbers, the hall ringing with music and laughter. I made my way through the throng, smiling a greeting here and there to people I passed. I loved to play the noble queen and enjoyed their respect, although deep down I knew it was more than I deserved.

'This time tomorrow Oswiu's fate will be all but sealed.' Penda leaned back in his chair, waving a leg of mutton. He took a large bite, chewing it open-mouthed. 'Ah,' he cried, catching sight of me, 'the night improves. Madam, I was just telling your husband that he must visit my Mercian holdings, you must accompany him.'

I smiled agreement. Cadafael had not greeted me but sat beside Penda, looking grimly at the floor. I guessed he was thinking of the morrow and my heart twisted a little. They were all soon to risk death; any one of them might ride away tomorrow, never to return. It was a threat we all had to learn to live with. There was never any real safety; none of us were truly secure.

Even I, a queen who had all the llys to do my bidding, could be dead by the following day of fever or misfortune. When I was a little girl, one of my maiden aunts with whom I had spent the afternoon, had choked to death at supper on a fish bone. It was the suddenness of her death that kept her in my memory, for the event had taught me that our time on earth was fleeting and that any one of us could be taken at any time. But, although we were all aware of life's impermanence, we did not dwell on it, but took pleasure as we found it, usually in small, unremarkable things.

From my seat, I surveyed the hall. It was a bigger crowd than I had ever known before. A crush of young men strutted hopefully before the maidens, children taunted hounds with scraps and, a little removed from the main company, the grandmothers sat huddled together, as hungry for gossip as for their supper.

At the end of the furthest bench my eyes fell upon Osian. He sat alone with a jug of mead at his elbow and I felt a twinge of pity which was quickly followed by an attack of exasperation. Why make such a fuss? What was done, was done. It was over and we must both move on. I was not really as heartless as this may sound, for although I didn't share his heartbreak, I did pity it. Time is a great healer and all this would pass. He was a good looking fellow and there were a hundred girls willing to salve his suffering, he would forget me soon enough.

Rhonwen came in and breathlessly took her place between Penda and I. I wondered if she could handle a man like that and hoped she would not become the focus to his attentions as I had been. I had noticed before that she ate capaciously at every mealtime, and when she began to enthusiastically fill our platters, I nibbled at a savoury to show willing although I was not in the least hungry.

I turned toward Cadafael, trying to catch his eye, my smile wide but he was not looking my way. Some instinct making me wary, I followed his eye to where Angharad wove her way through the throng toward him, her face aglow with triumph, and when I saw the look they exchanged, my heart plummeted, churning my stomach as I realised what should have been apparent from the first. All afternoon, while I had been absent with my son, she had been with Cadafael. That was why she had behaved so strangely on my return. That was why he could not look me in the eye.

I pushed my plate away and slumped back in my chair, my insides churning with misery and disgust, making me nauseous. I tried to act as if my husband weren't even in the room and fixed my gaze on the opposite end of the hall, where Osian sat. I had never felt so betrayed. I had truly believed all his talk of love, trusted in our newfound relationship but now he had spoiled it all and, at that moment, I felt I would never trust again.

It soon became impossible to hold back my tears and, when the first few drops fell, leaving a dark tell-tale spots on my bodice, I got up and made my way quickly from the hall. With a sick heart, I entered an antechamber, perched upon a stool and buried my head in my hands, openly weeping. I needed Ffreur, longed for her comfort, her sensible reasoning. She would have known how to prove my assumption wrong and reconcile me to the fact that I was loved and cherished by the man who had taken me as wife. When she was alive, I had taken her for granted, always supposing I was the strongest, the one who supported her but without her, I was as spiritless and as lost as a new-born babe.

'Heledd?' My head came up in time to see Osian close the door. He held up his hands to indicate he meant me no harm but I stood up, wary of his intentions and looked down my nose, wanting only to be alone with my misery.

'What do you want?' I sniffed and wiped my tears on my sleeve.

He took a step nearer. 'I want to say I am sorry. I want you to forgive me; I cannot bear it to end like this. I want you to be mine again.'

Turning astonished eyes upon him, I decided to tell him the truth. 'I never was yours, Osian, don't you understand that? You stole me from my brother's care when I was little more than a child, and then you made a cuckold of my husband but I was never yours. I never will be.'

'You hate me, then…' His voice trailed away, breaking with regret but it was no time to show the slightest sympathy so I shrugged and turned away. 'Oh, what does any of it matter? Just leave me alone.'

He took another step toward me but I threw up my arms before he came too close. 'I said, leave me.'

'Heledd, say you don't hate me and I will go.'

'I don't hate you.' My tone negated the meaning of the words, my voice flat and uncaring. In truth, I didn't hate him. I just craved some peace to sort out my feelings, wallow in my own tragedy.

'No, no,' he grabbed my hands. 'Say it and mean it, Heledd.' His face was close, his eyes awash with sorrow and, unwillingly, I felt myself relenting. I sighed and opened my mouth to speak but my words were cut off suddenly when the door flew open.

Cadafael took the floor in two strides toward us, his eyes blazing.

'Under my nose, Heledd?' he snarled before turning his fury on Osian who raised his hands in supplication.

'It isn't what you think, Lord, we did but discuss a suitable song for your entertainment.'

'You're a liar, minstrel.'

Before I could stop him, Cadafael raised his fist and, in a kind of trance, I watched the violence unfold. His fist smashed into Osian's jaw and sent him spinning to the floor. The events that followed seemed to be in slow motion, it didn't feel as if it was truly happening at all. I switched my eyes dully from one to the other, vaguely aware of imminent danger but too slow to act. My mind thick with shock, I tried to make sense of it all. What had made him suspect us? How could he know? He had never shown any sign of suspicion before. And then, as if in answer to my unspoken question, Angharad's upright figure appeared in the doorway.

She took her place at Cadafael's shoulder, her face fierce with triumph and I blinked at her for a while before shifting my gaze from her to Cadafael. The pain I saw in his eyes was like a physical blow and I knew then that I had lost him.

'My lord,' I stepped forward. 'I don't know what this woman has told you but it is lies. I have not betrayed you…would never betray …' My voice gave out on the lie.

Cadafael turned his bleak eye upon me and I thought I saw a glimmer of hope but then she laughed, and moved, like a serpent, toward me, her eyes glittering like a devil's as she circled me.

'Oh yes, she has, many times. Look, My Lord, is your son, Hedyn, not the image of this minstrel, this ... nobody? Does he not have the same eyes, the same hair? Don't you think that is not too strange to be a co-incidence?'

Her voice was honey-smooth. I wanted to kill her, to sink my nails into her evil, deceitful eyes and tear them from her head. Cadafael looked as if he would vomit. His face was like parchment, his eyes burning black against the pallor of his cheeks. He would not look at me, his chest was heaving. I reached out to grab his sleeve but he threw me off so that I almost fell. It was as I fought to regain my balance that he turned his fury upon Osian.

'I will kill you.' His voice was like cold water and no one doubted his words.

'Cadafael ...' My whisper was like a sigh as his sword left its sheath, I swallowed, searching for my voice, finding it quickly as violence erupted once more. 'Cadafael,' I screamed, 'he is unarmed.'

Time seemed to freeze, paralysing our bodies into effigies of stone. The weapon hovered for a few fateful seconds in the air above Osian's head, the blade burnished gold in the torch light. I clasped my hands, fell to my knees, my breath trapped in my lungs and begged him to hold his hand. It was a moment I will forever recall. Cadafael looked at me, with all the dishonour I had brought down upon him blazing from his eyes. One shining, screaming second and then his sword fell, silently and slowly, cutting through the solid air, severing the bonds of our marriage and slicing through Osian's heart.

Blood spurted forth. Great gouts of it. I scrambled on my knees toward him, trying to staunch the wound, my screams filling the chamber with men at arms.

I heard Cynddylan's angry voice. 'What goes on here? Cadafael? Heledd? Who has slain my minstrel?'

I could not speak or move. His head lay in my lap. His eyes were blind, his breath stilled, while his heart's blood soaked into my skirts and into the floor rushes around me. Cadafael lowered his sword and gave Cynddylan a ghastly stare.

'Ask my wife,' he spat. He hated me. My head lowered in torment as, with his pride in tatters he allowed Angharad to lead him away. Away from me. Away from our children.

'Wait.' It was Cynddylan's voice that halted them. 'You cannot just walk away. I am owed an explanation, Cadafael. You have murdered my servant.'

He was indignant, both at the violence that had broken all the rules of hospitality and the loss of a valuable asset. Cadafael turned, looked Cynddylan bleakly in the eye and shrugged, as if he did not care. 'Then I must explain that your sister is a whore and I, it seems, am a cuckold. She has degraded herself in the arms of your minstrel and passed his bastard off as my son.' His voice shook, my actions sounding the more terrible for being spoken aloud.

Faces turned to look at me, hands raised to mouths, followed by a murmur of surprise. I hated myself.

I wanted to die. I had betrayed them all.

Cynddylan was speechless.

But Cadafael was walking away. I had to stop him. I scrambled from beneath Osian's prone body, leaving him sprawled in his own gore, and hurried after them, careless of the gawping crowd, my voice rasping as I called his name.

'Cadafael. Please, let me explain, in the privacy of our chamber.'

He hesitated. For the first time he met my eye and the look he gave me triggered a dagger of despair. I have never seen a man so defeated. To my shame, I attempted a small regretful smile, hoping even at that late stage to sway him with my charm, and just for a moment I thought he would relent and listen to my explanation. But she stopped him. Angharad touched his arm and raised herself on tiptoe to whisper in his ear.

I had not thought he could look any more defeated but this time when he turned to face me again his eyes were rheumy with grief, his voice a painful rasp.

'So, Madam, you paid this girl to lure me from your bed? I am that repulsive?' He moved toward me, his brow both puzzled and injured, and to my annoyance Angharad came with him. He leaned so close I could smell the mead on his breath. 'For how long, wife, did you keep my concubine in your pay?'

I opened my mouth and shut it again, lowered my head and a tear dropped. 'Nay, Lord, it isn't like that. Let me explain.'

But I knew I was beaten and my voice when I spoke was no more than a whisper.

Suddenly angry again, he shrugged Angharad from his arm and thrust his face into mine, making me shrink away although I wished for nothing more than to be taken into his arms. 'Explain? God in Heaven, Heledd, the time for explanation is gone. I release you from our marriage. It is done, DONE.'

'Cadafael.' My scream surprised even myself. As he strode away I sprang forward, tears spouting, nose streaming. I clung to his arm. 'But I love you, Cadafael, if you will only listen.'

He tried to shake me off but I refused to release him, dangling on my toes, my pride perished but he wrenched himself from my grip and thrust me away, in the process, catching my nose with one of his arm rings. I fell. Blood gushed down my face and a gasp of horror rippled through the watching crowd.

I scrambled back up onto my feet. 'Wait, husband, please, listen.'

But he kept on walking.

And then Cynddylan was there, holding me back, silently urging me to show some pride. I leaked blood and tears onto his jerkin until he handed me a kerchief. 'Hush,' he soothed, 'I will follow after and speak to him, get him to listen. Maybe he will come round. Rhonwen, look after her.'

I opened my mouth, spittle at the corners. 'But he has denounced me before the whole court. He will never climb down from that.'

Cynddylan followed after my husband, my younger brothers crowding after him. 'Cadafael,' I heard him call and I hurried in their wake, holding the kerchief to my nose. My face was numb and, slowly and painfully, my lips and nose were beginning to swell. Cadafael stopped, half-turned and waited for my brothers to draw near.

Many men would have quailed at the sight of Pengwern's finest up in arms but Cadafael was no coward. He raised his arms and let them fall again to his sides. 'What would you have me do, Cynddylan? You would act no differently were you in my place.'

Cynddylan looked at his feet and then back at Cadafael. 'If I were you, I would remember that my wife's brothers are powerful allies and deadly enemies.' His voice was deadly quiet, his expression grim. Cadafael snorted humourlessly.

'You would turn against me? Break the treaty?'

'Heledd was part of that alliance, you have shamed her, broken your marriage.'

'She shamed herself!'

His words were loud and clear, the truth of them cutting me deep. Their faces were close together now, the tension between them tearing the company apart. Men began to separate, move away from new-found allies to stand with old ones. The llys was forming into factions and I realised then that I had started a war.

'Would you fight me, Cynddylan? You know I have the right of it.'

'Aye, I will fight you, Cadafael. You have turned my sister's name to mud with your lies. You listen to your whore but refuse to listen to the explanation of your wife.'

'The truth is in her eyes, Cynddylan.'

As I heard the sliding steel of my brother's withdrawing sword, and saw Cadafael throw off his cloak and reach for his weapon, I longed only for my own life to end.

Penda stepped forward. 'Cynddylan, think, man. We need Cadafael's army. Can't you kill him later? This marital breach can be healed, they always are and if it isn't, well, I have room for another wife.'

He leered at me in silent invitation and Cadafael snarled at him. Penda stepped forward, spat in the dust. 'Take us one at a time, friend. One at a time. I will fight you after Cynddylan has had his turn. If you live.'

I could not watch. The clash of their weapons eddied back and forth across the precinct. My personal household crept forward, gathering about me. At my shoulder Hild sniffled, her apron held to her face and Rhonwen's hand slipped through the crook of my elbow. She gave a squeeze of comfort, praying silently beneath her breath for the survival of her own man. I looked down at her closed eyes, her fervently furrowed brow and joined her, praying to Christ with more passion and less hope than I ever had before.

The watchers shuffled back as the fight came close, their feet scuffing up dust, their faces a kiss apart, weapons locked. Sweat poured from them, the stench of hatred rank in the air, their veins proud on their foreheads. It was a great trial of strength. Cyddylan was slighter than Cadafael but more agile and wiry against Cadafael's bulk.

Cynddylan broke free and backed off, wiped sweat from his eyes. Cadafael crouched over his sword, waiting for the next assault. There was blood in his beard but it was not clear if it were his own or my brother's. Whatever the outcome of this battle, there could be no victory for me. I loved them both. It was too much to bear.

As they began to fight again I ran forward, dragging Rhonwen with me. 'Please, stop,' I cried, although I knew it was hopeless. 'This will solve nothing.'

I reached out to grasp Cynddylan's tunic and he turned his head briefly, thrust me out of the way but, in that moment Cadafael's sword spliced my brother's sleeve, the scarlet stain spreading as quickly as a rumour.

I drew back, mortified at what I had done.

Cynddylan staggered, fell to his knee, a hand to his wound while Cadafael's weapon hovered above him. Sweat dripped from my brother's hair, his eyes riveted on the shining blade, waiting for it to strike. My heart banged loud. Rhonwen's fingers dug into my flesh as we watched open-mouthed, fear like vomit in our throats.

Then Cadafael put up his weapon. 'I have no hatred for you, man. I do not want to kill you. Let us stop now before further damage is done.'

I ran forward again. 'Yes, for the love of God, stop it now. Direct your anger toward Oswiu on the morrow, both of you.'

Cynddylan ignored me, pushing me away again. His face was a snarl as he spat on the ground. 'I will not fight you, Cadafael, but neither will I fight alongside you. Get out of my sight, for the next time we meet, you can be sure I will finish this.'

I had never heard such brutality in my brother's voice. I had only ever seen his regal side for usually he kept his savagery for the battlefield. His face was white in my defence.

Sheathing his sword, Cadafael jerked his head at Angharad and she ran to do his bidding. His hearth troop began to collect their belongings, call for their horses. People were moving away, they were leaving. I stood in the dust and saw my husband defeated not by battle, but by me and I thought I would never feel more sorry.

'Cadafael,' my head drooped but he was unmoved.

'Good day, Madam,' he said and, although I did not look up, I knew that he executed an ironic bow. I kept my head lowered, my heart breaking further as I heard his horse brought forward, the creak of leather as he mounted but I could not look up. I did not want to watch him leave me. But then I heard a voice.

'Where are we going, Father?'

My head shot up. 'NO!' The screams of a madwoman emerged from my mouth, all dignity forgotten. 'No, you can't do this, you can't do this.' I scrambled after the horses, trying to grab the trappings and haul them to a halt.

Cynfeddw was mounted before his father. He looked back at me, his face crumpled as though he would cry and, at that moment, when it was too late, I loved him with all my heart and soul. Angharad cradled my daughter. I could see the tufts of my little Ffreur's hair peeking from her blanket while Medwyl rode pillion behind her, clinging to her mother's waist. She waved a fat hand at me. 'Bye,' she called, thinking it all a happy jaunt.

'Wait,' I gasped for breath, running beside the horses, stumbling on the rutted track. 'Wait.' I appealed to her maternal instinct, clung to her stirrup. 'Angharad, I will give you anything, please, just let me have my daughter.'

Angharad sneered down me, finally letting me see the depths of her hatred. I grabbed her ankle. 'Please,' I sobbed, 'don't do this.' As the horses broke into a trot, she lifted her foot and struck me a stunning blow beneath the chin, sending me slumping into the dirt of Pengwern.

That was the last I ever saw of Cadafael, or our babies, and the memory I carry most clearly is of my family riding away, leaving me alone.

Eight

'Come, come inside, Heledd.' Gwarw's face was lined with grief but I turned away from her. I had not care for the sorrows of others. 'No, no, leave me. There is nothing to come in for.'

I heard her footsteps shuffling away but I remained were I was, weeping for all that was lost, my husband, my babies and my sister. There was nothing left.

I sat there for so long that the light began to fail. People passed me with lowered voices, unsettled to see their princess in the dust. When the sun began to sink into the distance the preparations for night began, just as if nothing had happened. Milkmaids hurried by with leather buckets and hens stopped scratching in the dirt about me and returned to their roosts in the barn. The torches were lit, their flickering light sneaking beneath the shutters and the aroma of roasting meat wafted toward me. But the smell did not make me crave nourishment. I thought I would never bring myself to eat again and so instead, it made me retch.

Then came a light footstep and a small, trembling hand upon my head. 'Mother?'

It was a long moment before I finally turned to find Hedyn, his face diluted with sorrow and besmirched with dirt and tears. I stared at him, slowly realising that I was not alone after all. I drew him into my breast and knowing he was all I had left, and I was all he had, we wept together, seeking comfort from our mutual loss.

'When shall we see them again, Mother? I have no playmates, now. I want Medwyl to come back.'

At dawn the armies of Powys and Mercia rode away, their expected numbers depleted by Cadafael's withdrawal. The noise of their departure dragged me from sleep and, for a few blissful moments, I forgot the horrors of the day before. But, as I inhaled the smoke from the brazier and blinked at the timbered ceiling, the memory trickled back, cleaving my heart afresh.

Not knowing what else to do I threw back the covers and shrugged myself into my cloak and crept to the bower door to watch the hearth troop ride away. I blinked in surprise at the women and children who cheered and waved as they rode out of the precinct. It was as if yesterday's disaster had never happened. It took me some time to realise that the tragedy had only happened to me, everyone else could live on. It was only I who lacked the will to do so.

The destruction of my life and marriage was just a passing event in the monotony of their lives. Soon they would forget all about it and I would just be Heledd the unfortunate, bereft of her children, forced to live on her brother's charity. The rest of my life would be spent in shame and regret. It was as well that Ffreur had not lived to see it.

Usually the sight of children lining the path of the cavalcade, their kerchiefs waving, trumpets sounding and dogs barking, would have filled me with a proud joy. I would have raised my own kerchief and run alongside, cheering with the rest, but that day I felt nothing, nothing but pain.

Cynddylan, his wound bound tightly, his face a shade paler than usual, raised a hand as he passed and tossed me a comforting smile. Then came Cynwraith and Cynon, with a salute for their errant sister. Their misguided faith in me sent a pang of guilt through my heart and I could not return their smiles but merely drew my cloak tighter. It came as some comfort that my brothers gave no credence to my disgrace but my mouth refused to turn upward and the best I could manage was a grimace.

Hedyn, fresh from his bed, slid his hand into mine. I looked down. His face was pinched, pink and white with sleepy sorrow but he raised a hand in farewell to his uncles, and I squeezed his fingers, proud of his sense of duty.

'You are chilled,' I drew him beneath my cloak, pressed him against my body, taking some comfort from his tiny frame. Then, as the last of the troop dwindled away and the supply wagons began to roll by, we turned into the warmth of my chamber.

Apart from the hole in my heart everything seemed so normal. I could almost believe Cadafael was off on some raid and would soon burst through the door and take me in his arms, laugh and kiss away my tears. All day I sat silently at the hearthside while Gwarw and Hild worked their needles but, try as I might, I could not rouse myself from misery although I knew I should do so for my child's sake.

I could not get warm and crept closer to the big cheerful flames with Hedyn curled like a youngling in my lap. He kept asking questions that I had no answer for.

'Why are you crying? Where has Father taken them? When are they coming back? Why do we not follow them?'

I wanted to scream at him to stop but, instead, I got up, set him on Hild's knee and rolled onto my bed to hide my face beneath my pillow. Then I wept again and after a while he came and watched me with his thumb in his mouth as if he were afraid that I was going to leave him too.

It was a terrible time of unrelenting misery. I decided that, on Cynddylan's return I would beg him to send to Cadafael, explaining, imploring forgiveness, asking him to try again, offering him payment … anything. It was not too late, some deep fundamental part of me told me that he loved me and, once the anger was gone, surely he would forgive.

I began to think up excuses in my head. Perhaps I could say I was bewitched or coerced, anything to vindicate myself, anything to keep him. But, each time I strung together a pretty sentence, it sounded specious, even to my ears and, in the end, I decided to merely tell the truth and hope for understanding.

As Gwarw is so fond of saying, there is a first time for everything.

Cynddylan's hunting bitch had whelped and Gwarw had taken Hedyn to see the pups and, taking advantage of the silence, I tried to sleep but every few minutes I woke with a start in my empty bed, with a hollow heart. The pain was like a hunger, a great yawning hole in my gut that would not let me rest. I continued to sleep in fits and starts all afternoon and when I finally got up it was late afternoon and coming on to dark.

My legs felt leaden as I swung them over the side of the bed and reached for my cup. I drank deeply, the cool ale refreshing my jaded pallet. The room was in shadow, the torches not yet lit but I spied a hearth wench knelt at the fire, quietly piling on fresh logs.

'Where is everyone?'

My voice was husky from too much sorrow. She jumped and turned her head toward me. 'Oh, Lady, you are awake. I think Gwarw has a plan to distract Prince Hedyn. He was so taken with the King's pups that she has gone to beg one from his steward. Hild is watching Hedyn as he sleeps, I believe. His dreams are troublesome. Are you hungry? Shall I send for a tray?'

Her face was so friendly and open that it was almost my undoing. I had thought everyone would hate me now my true nature had been revealed, but here she was, no more than eleven-years-old and as motherly as a broody hen. I opened my mouth to answer but the sound of a single galloping horse, coming straight into the enclosure and right up to the bower door stopped my words.

With a wild leap of hope in my heart I stood up, my eyes wide, a hand to my thumping chest. There came shouting and a scurry of footsteps and the chamber door was flung open.

Cadafael!

I leapt up from my seat, expecting him to stride through the portal and put an end to all this silliness but, as my eyes adjusted and I saw instead that it was only Cynddylan's page, Emyr, my heart sank. He staggered toward me, his jerkin split open, a dirt encrusted wound upon his chest and I saw that his message was dire indeed.

'Emyr. My Goodness, you are hurt. What tidings?'

I knew his news was ill before I had finished uttering the words. He fell to his knees, signalled desperately for a cup. Mine was half-full and I thrust it into his hand and burned with impatience as he let the cooling liquid flood down his throat.

He drew his sleeve across his mouth and took a deep breath, filling his lungs with courage. 'We must flee, Lady. We are defeated, the survivors few. Oswiu is victorious and rides against us even now.' His chest heaved, his words issuing in jerks and I could see from his expression that he had ridden through hell and back. 'Take the women and children into the hills, Lady, or Oswiu will take you as his slaves …or worse.'

I could not move. He was no more than twelve, his eyes red-rimmed with tears, his chin lacking a beard but he grasped my arm, breaching etiquette. 'Lady!' he yelled, shaking me a little. 'You must act now, before all is lost, think of your son.'

I managed to speak at last. 'My brothers?'

'Cynddylan and Gwion still live. They are at the gate with their troop, strengthening the outer defences. I know nothing of the others. Lady, you must hurry.'

Still I did not move.

'What of Penda and his armies? Surely he lives?'

The boy bowed his head, shook it sorrowfully from side to side. 'Nay, Lady, the fighting was vicious. I saw King Penda go down in the fray, his war axe taking with him as many as he could.'

It was not possible. Not Penda, the savage King of Mercia. He could not be dead. I gave a disparaging laugh that emerged as a sort of sob. It was not possible, my head repeated over and over. Not the warrior King Penda, surely?

Leaping into action, I ran barefoot from the chamber shrieking for Gwarw and Hild before diving into the antechamber where Hedyn slept on a makeshift pallet. Hild was with him and as I crashed into the room she leapt to her feet. 'Whatever is the matter, are you sick?'

Her mouth gaped as I gabbled a version of Emyr's story.

'Oh, my lord,' Hild began to grizzle, picking up Hedyn's jerkin, tearing off his covers, shaking him awake and forcing his sleepy arms into his sleeves. If I had had time I would have worried more about my son's passive acceptance of the wild events that were taking shape. Unfortunately, there was no time, not then nor afterwards.

'Come,' I cried. 'There is no time.'

We fled, half-dressed, from the hall, speeding across the chaotic enclosure to the outer gate where Cynddylan was barking out instructions to his men, who were shoring up the defences, assembling missiles to launch onto the enemy.

When he saw me Cynddylan scrambled down from the rampart, and I saw that one side of his face was caked in blood, a gaping wound on his cheekbone. That won't help his looks, I thought irrationally before I was shaken again, this time by my King.

'Heledd,' he grabbed my arm. 'Take your women and the children...' Belatedly he remembered that I only had one left, '... and your son, to the hills. Stay there until you hear the horn sound. Do not come down until you are summoned. Not for anything, do you hear me?'

I nodded and for once I did not argue. Emyr ran beside me. I gripped Hedyn's hand, hitched my skirts and dragged him up the hillside, behind me the women followed, as fast as they were able. I could hear them gabbling in panic and, when I stopped suddenly, they ran into my back, almost knocking me down. I had been struck by a thought and it was not a happy one. I turned and grabbed the page's arm.

'How long do we have, Emyr?'

He shrugged. 'A few hours, no more. We rode like the devil ahead of them.'

I thought rapidly, licking my lips. I had enough on my conscience. 'Take my women and my son to the hillside. Stay out of sight until danger is past. I must alert the others, help my aunts and uncles, the children, rouse the servants, free the slaves or they will all perish.'

He bridled, his juvenile face full of manly outrage. 'You will do no such thing, Lady. Someone else will rouse them. You must take your women and Hedyn and get yourself to safety. The King gave strict orders. I cannot let you disobey them.'

I set my chin, refused to budge and did not miss the glimmer of admiration that kindled in his eye. After a few moments of stalemate he drew himself up to his full height, almost reaching my shoulder. 'You go on, Madam. I will go myself and bring them after. Do not worry.'

And, before I could argue, he had sprinted away, his little head bobbing among the brambles.

After sending up a prayer for his protection, I led my women onward. It was a weary climb and my limbs craved rest. Only fear drove me onward. We climbed, higher than I had ever gone before, to where the undergrowth was dense and the scree difficult to negotiate.

Gwarw, uncharacteristically weeping, hobbled behind me, each footstep an agony while Rhonwen and Hild urged her to hurry. My poor, faithful Gwarw, who had been the mainstay of my life, battling with her swollen, chilblained feet against the need for haste. I urged them onward, cursing like a scold to keep them moving. With cruel and scathing words I drove them on, telling myself I would make it up to them later. My women had suddenly become invaluable to me, something to protect and hold on to if it cost me my life, but now was not the time for kindness.

At last, to everyone's relief, we huddled in the shelter of a large outcrop where scrub grew up to screen us from the enemy below. If I stood on the tip of my toes, I could just see the llys far below us, and the river running into the flooded valley and on toward the sea.

From our great height the skerries looked tiny and the men milling about them as small and as insignificant as insects, although I knew that each and every one of them had a family and home. I suppose, when seen en mass, we all appear as nothing more than insects; our approaching enemy had no concept of us as people who wept and loved and laughed. We were just in their way, like a nest of wasps and so must be destroyed. I think that was the moment, although I had not the time to contemplate it, that I first conceived the true cost of war.

I scanned my eye in the other direction, across the purpling mountaintops until I perceived, in the distance, a cloud of dust far off on the valley road. 'They are coming,' I whispered and Rhonwen began to cry, her head in Gwarw's chest, the old woman patting her shoulder, crooning comfort as she so often had to me. I turned away from them, into the wind. I could offer them no consolation, would make them no false promises. In the next few hours anything could happen.

And then, quite suddenly, as if from nowhere, an eagle flew down, the wind from his wings lifting my hair, his mournful cry penetrating something buried deep within my mind, bringing the memory of heartbreak and defeat. And pain and dread lurched in my stomach as I recollected a childhood dream.

I looked up at the wheeling eagles, real this time and, certain what was to come, I fell to my knees, begging Ffreur's God with all my heart, not to let it happen.

The night was long, and cold. I crouched with my women, cradling my son in my arms. We were hungry, thirsty and afraid. I did not sleep but sat a little apart from the others, watching as the sun clambered over the horizon to herald the dismal day.

It was not long after dawn that we heard the far-off clash of swords, and distant cries of anguish. I untangled myself from Hedyn's clinging hands to look down to the llys, dreading that which I knew I would see.

I could not discern faces but could clearly see tiny figures on horseback striking down those who fought on foot, the cries of the injured, like the mews of a new-born kitten, drifting, helpless toward us.

I remembered Cadafael saying that Oswiu would take no prisoners.

Soon a Judas wind bore the acrid stench of smoke, fanning the flames, hastening the destruction of Cynddylan's Hall. Gwarw and Hild blubbered like children behind me while Hedyn sat quiet in Rhonwen's lap, his head laid upon her breast, passive, accepting ... flaccid, but I had no time to worry for him.

Poor Gwarw, who had driven mercilessly uphill the evening before, was suffering badly. Her feet were still bleeding and muddy from the climb and her hair hung in grey knots about her face, making her seem suddenly much older. If I did not take care of her, I would lose her next.

'Here, let me see.' I crouched to examine her wounds, wishing we had thought to bring water and, tearing a strip from my petticoat, I began to bind them, promising a salve when the crisis was passed.

'Thank you,' she said. She had looked after me since the day I was born yet here she was, clinging to my hand, her old woman's tears falling, reversing our roles, and for once dependent upon me. I patted her hand and stood up, screwing up my face as I wondered what on earth we were to do.

I was too afraid to go down until the summons came and so we waited there all day and through the next night, never knowing how the battle went. 'The horn will sound soon,' I assured them. 'Don't worry.'

But it was long in coming, and the longer we waited the greater our fear became until each rustling goat in the undergrowth became a potential enemy, each swift bird a deadly missile.

It was noon the following day when, my lips parched, my belly growling, I peered down to the llys again. I could see no movement at all but it was plain the royal palace was a ruin. Smoke billowed from the remains of the feasting hall and the charred timbers of the ladies bower stretched in a lament to the leaden sky. The buildings smouldered, the blackened roof joists rearing like a huge skeleton to the smoke choked clouds. Nothing stirred, only the flap of rags and the shifting shadows of the passing day.

I knew that death awaited us there and at last, disobeying Cynddylan's last request, I faced the fact that I must go down to face yet more sorrow and bear witness to my penance.

'Come,' I said, turning to the women. 'I think it is safe now.'

The hall had been high and proud, a place of feasting, symbolic of Pengwern's invincible power, a place that tales were told of. A place to which men travelled from afar. Now, it lay in ruins and my women and I walked among ashes and blackened timbers.

I stood in the great hall and looked up through the place where the roof had been to the empty heavens above. Beneath my feet the debris of my life lay crushed and broken, to be blown by the wind and extinguished by squalling rain until Pengwern and the people who lived there were forgotten.

Just one bower, less damaged than the others, remained standing, the charred door swinging, drunkenly on its great hinge. I tried to push it open but something lay against it, hindering my progress. With much pushing and heaving I managed to make a small gap and, leaving Gwarw and the others poking dismally in the ashes, I slid through and into void beyond.

I can barely speak of what I found there. It was too pitiful for tears. I stood, dry-eyed, looking down upon what was left of our people. At their head lay Emyr, still clutching his sword, his lips drawn back, his teeth bared, his eye sockets plundered by carrion. His corpse was sprawled across the smouldering bodies of my aunts and uncles, those whom I had sent him to liberate and who he had protected till his last breath. That small brave boy had given up his life to save their souls.

The sparrow-thin limbs of our elders were twisted and broken, their arms naked of rings, plundered by the victors. My uncle Borian, recognisable only by the sword he still held aloft had striven to protect his women. This was no proper end for an old warrior, and although I could not tear my eyes away, it was hard to look upon the rage that death had frozen onto his features. I removed my shawl and laid it across him with a whispered prayer.

All around me, as I waded on through the corpses of my kin, the eagles feasted like devils on their flesh. I had to stop them. I called the others for help and they came at once, my depleted retinue, pushing through the gap in the door, crying out aloud at the pitiful sight that waited on the other side. We were nothing now but a pathetic huddle of stricken women and one small boy, and every one of them was looking to me for guidance.

Me. Heledd the adulterer, who had no answers.

Our burdened hearts aching, we pulled our loved ones from the embers and piled their blackened, brittle bones into a shallow grave. Our faces became daubed with their funeral dust and so hot was the ground beneath us that the skin was melted from our feet. Our task was beyond sorrow and we worked on in deathly silence, a prayer on every lip to a God that none of us were sure was listening.

Rhonwen found Cynddylan first. I heard her cry out, saw her fall to her knees in the ashes and knew without being told what she had discovered. I stood beside her and looked down at my brother, the battle standard she has stitched for him had become his funeral shroud. He was burned black by the fires of war and just one arm remained untouched by the raging flames, the arm of the hand that bore the royal ring of Pengwern.

Keeping my eyes averted from the thing that had been my dearest brother, my honoured King, I went on my knees and drew the ring from his finger. Then I called my son to me. Hedyn was the last remaining link to Pengwern and as far as the world was concerned he was Cynddylan's heir. As I pushed the ring of Pengwern over the knuckles of a minstrel's child and made him swear to seek vengeance, my throat closed in misery.

'You are Pengwern's King now, my son,' I said. He made no reply, so I gave him a little shake, 'You must take vengeance for this when you are a man.' He nodded uncomprehendingly, and looked at me, his face white beneath the grime, his eyes awash with the sort of fear that no child should ever know.

The sort of fear that is never erased.

I stood up, keeping hold of Hedyn's hand and looked about me for the last time upon the ruin of my dynastic home. Nothing was left. No people, no treasures, no land, no authority, all was laid waste. Pengwern would never rise again.

Ffreur's laughter was silenced, and the throne stood empty, the army obliterated and, knowing myself to be solely to blame, I looked upon my slaughtered kin and our derelict hall and thanked God that Ffreur had not lived to see it.

PART SIX
HELEDD'S HYMN

The Hall of Cynddylan pierces me
Every hour, after the great gathering din at the fire
Which I saw at thy fire-hearth!

The hall of Cynddylan is dark tonight. Those words are like a wasp in my head, stinging and cruel and I cannot lose the memory. I do not sleep, only doze and pray, and doze again, no difference between day and night. I remember a poem that Osian once sang.

For a while the leaves are green,
then they turn yellow,
fall to earth and die,
crumbling to dust.

The leaves of my father's tree have withered in their prime, and it was I who wielded the axe and struck the first blow. I will never forgive myself for the consequences of my girlish infatuation, and of all the passions that raged through my young body, the love, the anger, and even the grief, now there is only shame remaining … and the guilt.

God will never forgive me. I have tried hard to make recompense but my crimes eats away at me like a great stinking canker for which there is no cure.

I regret so much.

My women and I travelled for many months, our bellies empty, and our feet sore. As I had feared, it was all too much for Gwarw, her poor old feet could no longer carry her and she perished at the roadside early one morning, clinging to my hand, begging my forgiveness, but for what, I do not know. Throughout my entire life she nagged, slapped, cosseted, and bullied me into being a good person but it seems I didn't have it in me. I am to blame for it all. As we lay her in her shallow, makeshift grave, my already shattered heart fragmented a little more, and the only comfort I could find was the knowledge that she was better off dead. I hoped she was with Ffreur now, somewhere where sorrow is a stranger and tears are never shed.

After that, my companions left me one by one. When Hild grew too sick and weak to continue I gave her into the care of a small group of nuns but I could not stay, although they would have welcomed me. I was driven to travel onward, compelled to keep walking and I would not stop for, at each stop on our journey, every time I began to feel better, the faces of Pengwern's murdered people came back to haunt me. They would not let me rest and so I kept walking although I had no direction. And one day there was just Hedyn and I, a ragamuffin princess and the son of singer of songs.

What a sorry pair.

Hedyn was not the boy he had once been. Cynddylan's ring hung heavy on his skinny finger. He clutched at it, looking anxiously about him as if he feared King Oswiu were hidden behind every bush. His fearful eyes came to disturb me as surely as the dead ones of his father and uncles. He clung to my skirts, trudging alongside me, rarely speaking and never complaining but I knew that all his joys had perished. All our hopes burned up in the fires that had raged through Cynddylan's hall.

In the end Osian's son fell sick of the fever when he was but twelve years old, and although I nursed him as best I could, he too was taken from me. His short life had been a sorry one and I was solely to blame for that too. I would have done better to make sure he was never born at all than to damn him to the life he had.

Alone, I laid him beneath the soft sod and added his memory to my other sorrows, and thereafter whispered his name in my many prayers.

Since then, I have spent a lifetime alone at this small stark church at the head of the valley. It is a pretty place that looks down across the land to the place where the setting sun sparkles on the surging sea. The local people call it Heledd's church, although in truth, it is God's church, not mine.

I am old now. I did not deserve the reward of an early death but it will come soon now. These days my hands tremble, the skin on them is spotted with age and those same breasts that once so enchanted Osian and Cadafael knock like empty pouches against my ancient ribs.

I have been a bad person and although I have prayed for many years I still cannot believe that God forgives me, and until that time I will find no peace. Thirty years of prayer is not enough to expiate my sins and so deep is my guilt that I if lived until the World's end it would not be long enough to expunge my crimes with prayer.

I am not afraid of death. The only fear I have is that even when I am laid within my oaken coffin I will not rest easy but will continue to walk this sorry world, cut off from heaven and all that I love. I am the last survivor, and when I am gone there will be no one left to pray for the poor perished people of Pengwern. That is why I inscribe these parchments now, in the hope that whosoever finds them will continue to pray for Ffreur, and for Cynddylan and perhaps just a little, for me.

Often of a night, when ague shakes my old bones and my knees are stiff from the kneeling, I let my mind remember Ffreur and how joyful things once were. I am shamed by my youthful sorrows that seem so trite and shallow in the face of true grief. It makes me cringe to remember the self-righteous young girl I was. With each new trial God sent, I thought it was the worst that could ever be. I did not learn that lesson until I had lost everything.

I was a fool. My marriage should have been a blessing yet I saw it only as a curse. My first born should have been an answered prayer yet was merely a burden. And my wifely duties that should have brought me joy, brought only revulsion.

And my lies, my egocentric deceptions, which I had regarded as cunning, all ended in ruin … not just for me … but for everyone. What a silly, vain, headstrong thing I was, and how unfit to be a princess, let alone a queen.

If only I could change the past.

My story began and ended with Ffreur. She was the better, purer half of me, and I wish I had heeded her inborn wisdom. Sometimes, as I sit here in the dark, I feel her loving arms slip around me, her breath tickling my ear, her laughter warming my frigid world.'

'Sing to me, Heledd,' she says and her presence cheers me a little and I sing her my refrain once more, knowing that it makes her smile to hear it.

> My name is Heledd and this has been my song. Please sing it.

Author's Note

This novel, The Song of Heledd is a work of fiction inspired by fragments of Welsh poetry known as Canu Heledd and Marwnad Cynddylan. The poem, and others relating to Heledd and Pengwern, can be found in the Red Book of Hergest which is housed in the University of Oxford's Bodleian Library. The Red Book of Hergest dates from the 14-15th centuries but the poems themselves are believed to have been written in the 9th century, although set in the 7th. Canu Heledd seems to be part of an older oral tradition, recorded and transcribed in the medieval period.

Canu Heledd is a cycle of saga englynion in which Heledd is the narrator. Apart from this poem, there are very few female dialogues in the saga tradition and Jenny Rowlands in her book Early Welsh Saga Poetry extends this, saying, 'women do not speak or appear, and even allusions to their existence is rare. '

Sole survivors of disaster are not uncommon in saga poetry but female survivors are. This dispensing with tradition suggests to me that Heledd's story is perhaps a true one, a historical event that has passed down through the oral tradition to become legend.

Heledd is the sole surviving member of the royal house of Pengwern. Her dynasty and family have been destroyed and, in the poem, her brother, King Cynddylan's, hall is in ruins. Her lament for him and the destruction of the royal seat remains powerfully emotive, but the thing that struck me the most is her sense of blame.

It seems that her actions have brought about the downfall of the dynasty and she is unprepared to forgive herself. The poem itself is historically inaccurate, written for entertainment not to enter the historical record but the combined documents make fascinating reading, each complementing the other.

Historically we know nothing about Heledd herself but her brother, Cynddylan is believed to have united with Cadafael of Gwynedd and Penda of Mercia against Northumbrian forces in the battles of Maes Cogwy, Chester, Lichfield and Winwaed, where Penda was slain.

Shortly after Winwaed in 655AD Oswiu invaded Mercia and Powys, launching an attack upon the royal llys at Pengwern and practically obliterating the dynasty in one night.

It has been suggested that, in order to cement the alliance between Powys and Gwynedd, Heledd acted as a peaceweaver and was married to Cadafael, then King of Gwynedd.

For reasons we will never know, on the eve of the battle at Winwaed, Cadafael suddenly withdrew his troops and rode back to Gwynedd, abandoning Powys and Mercia to their fate. This act earned him the title of Cadafael Cadomedd, which translates as 'battleshirker.' There is no record as to his motivation but it did his reputation little good and shortly afterward, although the circumstances remain sketchy, the rule of Gwynedd passed back to Cadwaladr.

In a small hamlet of Llanhilleth in the hills above Blaneau Gwent is a small church dedicated to St Illtyd. Mary of Monmouth, who writes a splendid blog, says of the church. 'Although currently dedicated to St Illtyd, the original dedication of the church was to St. Heledd or Hyledd, as evidenced by parish lists of the 16th and 17th centuries (Baring-Gould 1911, 254). This gave the place-name Llanhyledd of which Llanhilleth is an anglicised form.'

The historical detail of 7th century Powys and Gwynedd is very sparse. We can never know what really became of Heledd and her family but there are enough references to know they existed. The poems tell us that the family bond was strong, that Heledd was a woman whose actions impacted upon the world around her. The poem provides rich descriptions of the llys and the people who lived there, Cynddylan in his purple cloak, the richly carved mead halls, the merging tradition of Celtic and Christian religion. And the mention of Ffreur, a sister she once mourned but mourned no longer. Canu Heledd raises many questions but this one is the greatest. Heledd no longer mourns her sister? Why?

I spent many months sifting through the smoke-ruined embers of Cynddylan's hall to piece together a story for Heledd and Ffreur, a fiction of what might have been.

If you've enjoyed this book please consider leaving a short review.

Judith Arnopp's books are available in paperback, Kindle and some titles are on Audible.

author.to/juditharnoppbooks

The Beaufort Chronicles: the Life of Lady Margaret Beaufort (comprising of)
The Beaufort Bride
The Beaufort Woman
The King's Mother
The Heretic Winds: The life of Mary Tudor, Queen of England
Sisters of Arden: on the Pilgrimage of Grace
A Song of Sixpence: the story of Elizabeth of York and Perkin Warbeck
Intractable Heart: the story of Katheryn Parr
The Kiss of the Concubine: A story of Anne Boleyn
The Winchester Goose: at the court of Henry VIII
The Song of Heledd
The Forest Dwellers
Peaceweaver

Printed in Great Britain
by Amazon